WHERE IS
SAM

Davin

I hope you enjoy
my book

Bob F

Robert Frey

PAGE PUBLISHING, INC.
New York, NY

First originally published by Page Publishing, Inc. 2017

ISBN 978-1-64082-619-9 (Paperback)
ISBN 978-1-64082-620-5 (Digital)

Printed in the United States of America

INTRODUCTION

Emily Carson is an elementary schoolteacher married for ten years to a real estate broker named Sam. One day Sam unexpectedly vanished. She picked up the missing person's case of her husband when local police were unable to come up with any results and they closed the file. She hired a private investigator to help her find out what happened to Sam and why. What she learned along the way about her husband's family was disturbing. He never spoke of his past or his childhood. She went on a life-altering experience in a quest of solving the disappearance. She placed her life in harm's way by what she discovered and what she had to do to protect her life. From the FBI to the organized crime family of her husband, she navigated through one deception after another. She met David Kimbro and learned more about herself and how far she would go to survive.

CHAPTER ONE

Emily Carson woke in a sweaty, fitful state. She was dreaming about the desperate search for her lost husband when a loud banging sound filled her room. She looked at her alarm clock. It was 3:36 in the morning. Her husband has been missing for three months, with no indication of foul play or any kidnapping ransom demands. He had simply vanished. He was a successful real estate broker, seemingly in a happy marriage. Money could not be a motive for his disappearance or kidnapping because they had a modest income and were, by far, not wealthy. The only cause Emily could even bring herself to consider was an unaccountable misfortune. Maybe he suffered an accident and had amnesia. She felt he was out there somewhere. He was never involved in any unethical real estate transactions that she was aware. He was an honest and trustworthy man. If his disappearance was planned, there was no indication in their home, bank accounts, or other possessions. All his clothes were in the closet. His travel bags were still there and all his shoes. If there was another woman involved, surely she would have picked up on that. His routines were predictable. He was always organized and very detailed in his work and home life. Emily got out of bed and looked out of her window and saw the garbage truck picking up on their weekly route. For the last three months, her days had been filled with trying to make sense of the whole situation. The police had dismissed the case as one of many missing-persons complaints filed and is not one of their priorities for investigation.

Emily is an elementary special education teacher with a master's degree in special education. She is working with fifteen highly autistic students who occupy most of her day, which is a relief from the constant strain of dealing with her husband's disappearance. During the evenings, she constantly goes over and over the variables that would have led to his disappearance. Hiring a private detective is an option but can be expensive. Emily has spent many lonely nights questioning her plight. How long can she continue her life without her lifetime partner? At last, out of desperation, she makes a decision. With little money and lots of time after school, she starts her own investigation into his disappearance.

Little did she know what dark secret path she would have to explore to get some answers. She started to trace back every habit that she could remember that her husband Sam had. Hoping to stumble on any shred of information that could be a lead, she started with the police files. His last known whereabouts was in his office the evening he disappeared. She searched every inch of the office for any lead of what could have led to his disappearance. It turned up nothing. She did notice that his briefcase, which he always carried with him, was still on his desk. She looked through the files in the briefcase and still found nothing to tie into his sudden disappearance. The real estate market had become very erratic, and Sam was putting in late hours in an attempt to gain more clients and to open new, potential marketing areas. She noticed a receipt in the corner of his desk blotter. It was dated the night before his disappearance for dinner from a place she did not recognize: Labella's Italian Restaurant with a card attached with the name Joey Pataglia, and a phone number on the back. The card was from the restaurant on Third and McClure in the downtown area, twelve miles from the office. It is an upscale and expensive restaurant for dinners and special events. Emily thought it was strange that Sam never mentioned frequenting the restaurant, let alone whom he went there with or what client he had. Suddenly a cold chill went up her back as she recalled some time ago reading about a scandal involving a small-time crime boss named Joey Pataglia. *What connection existed between this man and my husband?*

Did my husband get involved in a transaction or some kind of a deal with this unsavory character?

Emily and Sam had been married for ten years and a long time ago had given up on having any children. Their marriage was a fairly close relationship, and both tried to devote their free time to each other. They were best friends. Unable to have children, Emily uses her job as a teacher to fill the hole she feels since they were childless. She's an attractive blonde woman in her midthirties, with a radiant personality. She has captured the cliché' of being cute, pretty and beautiful at the same time. Depending on her mood you can see one or all these qualities. She is a special person who has compassion and love for teaching and communicating with special needs students, while commanding respect and attention from her students. Now alone, she mulls over the unfortunate state of not having a child.

With the only possible lead being the receipt from Labella's Restaurant and the name on the card, Joey Pataglia, Emily set out to investigate any possible connections to Sam. The first thing she did was to go and see the detective, Tim Becket, who handled the missing person's case. She told him of her discovery, but he was quick to discredit any findings involving the restaurant and Mr. Pataglia, and backed off any further discussions on the subject. He strongly advised her to not pursue in that direction and told her not to go there. He indicated that she could get involved with the wrong parties and any accusations on her part could be dangerous. These are not the people to be asking questions to or about. Bewildered by his attitude, Emily felt a sudden sickness in her stomach and the blood drained from her head. She almost fainted. What did I hit on? Did I open a wound or a can of shit? This man was telling me that Joey Pataglia was untouchable. This was crushing. The only possible lead I had was being dismissed by the lead detective in my husband's disappearance.

CHAPTER TWO

Sam was in his late thirties, in good shape, and posed a very professional appearance and demeanor. He is of Italian and German descent. In May 1900, at the tender age of nineteen, Sam's maternal grandparents packed their belongings and set sail for America to start a new life. Over the course of twenty years, Carmella birthed seventeen children, two died young due to complications. That left the family with seven boys and eight girls. Sam's mother was the fourteenth of the fifteen surviving children. They settled in as all immigrants during that time period with their own countrymen in their own communities. Everyone pitched in and the neighborhood took care of their own kind. The Great Depression caused many critical decisions that had to be made by families in order to survive under duress conditions. Because of their vulnerability and lack of any other connections and in order to survive, the family became protected by the Black Hand, the ruling force of power for protection from outsiders and the law. Trust and loyalty to each other were a major influence and everyone scratched each other's backs. Many of the old ways were brought over from the homeland and enforced in their social network and behavior. Sam's mother's seven brothers, as they grew, soon became members of the ruling hand and started doing anything to gain money, notoriety, and possessions, in order to position themselves for a better life. Times were tough. The only law they understood was the law of survival and the ruling demands of those of the so called mob leaders. Petty theft, larceny, burglary, intimidation, prostitution, illegal betting, and gambling were the avenues to the riches sought to relieve the pressure of surviving the times. All seven brothers developed their own skills for survival and developed into successful businessmen. One brother, Samuel, ran and owned a construction company that received many lucrative contracts through his contacts from the old neighborhood.

Another brother, Frank, had a very successful insurance company and it was the top selling agency in the state. All his business contacts once again came from the organized crime families he was affiliated with in his youth. Still another brother, Alberto, became one of the family's attorneys, representing high profile suspected crime bosses. The other four were employed through the organization as collectors, union representatives, and operated car dealerships for the organization. All were very successful because they operated within the frame of the family and made all the so-called investor's large amounts of money.

Sam went to college by working and paying his own way. His uncles approached him numerous times offering to foot the bill for tuition in exchange he'd have to study corporate and real estate law to represent family in their various transactions. Sam refused. He wanted to make his own way and did not want to have a life time obligation to his family. He knew how his uncles had prospered. He heard all the conversations as a young boy at the family Sunday gatherings while having an Italian home cooked meal when he was a young boy. He would hide in the hallway when all the brothers would meet in the den to bring each other up to date on all the activities and upcoming plans for the week. He heard them conspire, scheme, and calculate every move and initiate their strategy to provide for and protect all their interests.

At that time, Sam had no idea of the gravity and effect these men imposed on others' lives. As he matured he began to understand what he had heard during those Sunday family gatherings.

Emily knew that she was on her own. The police had dismissed the case as another lost or runaway incident. What detective Becket did know, if anything, he was not willing to share. She was going all in. Risky or not, she had to know, Emily thought. She could feel it in my bones. Sam was out there and was waiting for her to find him, one way or another. She could not accept never seeing him again. He had to be alive. His disappearance was too cut and dry to be true. No phone calls. No messages to me. No activity on his credit cards. Nothing was missing from the house. The police could not even find his car. No sign of foul play. Her next step was to visit his last known location, and that was the Labella Italian Restaurant. How could she go undetected? What if he did meet foul play there and they recognized her? She could put herself in danger. It would look funny if she went alone, unescorted. That would raise questions and possible suspicions. She needed to figure out a way to go and not be noticed.

Maybe I should dye my hair, Emily thought. If he did meet foul play and this was planned, they may already know what I look like and this could scare off any advantage of my going there. Emily's mind raced as she calculated her options. *Who could I ask to go with me? Can I involve someone else? What do I look for when I do go? What questions do I ask? Maybe I should hire a private investigator.* Lying in bed that night, Emily decided the safest avenue to take was to seek help by hiring an investigator, no matter the cost. She would research and make calls the next day to find one.

CHAPTER THREE

David answered his phone, "Kimbro speaking, how may I help you?" The woman on the other end sounded tired and sullen, which is about the same way most of his calls come. She said she was looking for a reputable private investigator and he was the first one she wanted to interview. He asked her how she found him, on Craig's list, and laughed? She said no, but she did research him on the internet and he had favorable comments. He laughed again and thanked her for sharing that information. "What are you looking for?" She said she needed help in a missing person's case. "Who is the missing person?" he asked. My husband, she replied. Not another one he thought. "How long has he been missing?"

She replied, "Going on four months." This could be easy money. Usually the husband has bolted, has a new identity and is far, far, away. I could take her money, take her info, sit back, and wait until she becomes discouraged and gives up the search. He asked her the standard questions. "Did you file a missing person's report with the police?" She said yes. "Are they still active on the case?" he asked.

"No," was her comment.

That figures, he thought. Something in her voice caught his interest. She did not sound like the typical airhead he usually gets calls from for husbands gone missing. He probed her further by asking what she has done on her own and if she has any indication of why he left. She hesitated for a few seconds and said she may have a possible lead into his disappearance but could not handle it on her own. Wow, he thought. This woman could prove to be either smart or dangerous or both. "Well, since I am first on your list, let's meet and see if your lead is a viable one, then we can both make a decision on whether we can work together." She liked his suggestion. He at least said we could work together, which was encouraging after her dismissal by detective Becket. They arranged a meeting for the next evening at a local restaurant. After all, she wanted to meet him in a public place, see his ID, and his license to verify what he advertised he is.

It was seven o'clock and Emily sat in a corner waiting for David Kimbro to appear. She was dressed in a blue blouse and designer jeans. He said he would be wearing a navy blue polo shirt and khaki pants. He came through the door at exactly seven o'clock and she was struck with his clean shaven, clean cut appearance, and trim, fit body. He appeared to be about the same age as her. She expected an older man with wrinkled clothes and a shabby beard. David introduced himself and sat down across from her. He anticipated her wanting to see his identification and showed her without her having to ask. Another good point in his favor. They ordered dinner, then she proceeded to fill David in on all the information and up to date events of her husband's disappearance. When she finished, she asked him what would his fee be. David told her he charges by the hour, as do attorneys, because of the uncertainty of how long the case could take to solve or dissolve. His rate was seventy-five dollars an hour, plus any expenses of traveling out of the city. He said he would need a five hundred dollar retainer fee up front. Emily asked him how many active cases he was working on now. He said he usually has about five cases going at the same time but places priorities on each one as different events occur with each case. A lot of his work is high class society women cheating on their husbands. He has other missing person cases also. Usually I get called before months have gone by and the trail goes cold on a missing person. As they finished eating, David suggested that Emily think about whether she wants to pursue the case with him. He gave her his card, paid for the meals and said to give him a call if she decides to use his services.

Not what I expected, thought Emily. *He has a gentle demeanor, seems very professional, not to mention his good looks, and his fees seem reasonable.* For the first time in a long time, Emily felt like she may get the help she needed to find her husband.

CHAPTER FOUR

Sam was working late when he received a call from a potential client on the night before his disappearance. The man told Sam that he was interested in a property, and Sam was referred by a business acquaintance. He asked if Sam would be interested in representing his interest in a major transaction.

"Where is the property, and how much is the asking price?" Sam asked. The man said that he did not want to divulge that information over the phone. The potential client then asked Sam if he could join him for a late dinner down town at Labella's Italian Restaurant at eight o'clock. Sam asked the man his name. Mr. Jones was the reply. Excited over the prospect of being in on a large deal made it an easy decision. He would meet Mr. Jones at eight. He was thinking of calling Emily and telling her of the big opportunity but wanted to surprise her when it fell into place.

Sam parked his car in the lot next to the restaurant and walked in the building. The interior was immaculate with an upscale and very expensive decor. He was greeted at the door and asked for Mr. Jones. He was told that Mr. Jones was expecting him and the waiter escorted him to a table where two men were sitting. A distinguished gentleman rose and greeted Sam with a firm handshake. The man had on a tailored, form fitting, expensive suit and his hair was styled. He looked like he just stepped out of Gentlemen's Quarterly. The other man sat in his chair and nodded. He was a large, bulging man who looked like an enforcer you see in movies.

"What would you like to drink?" asked Mr. Jones.

Sam declined, saying he has had a long day and a lengthy ride home.

"Then let's order dinner and we can talk," suggested Mr. Jones. While waiting for their dinner to arrive, Mr. Jones quizzed Sam about his real estate background. He also said that the investment of the property they are interested in is one of many his group would like to procure. He is looking for someone to represent his group of investors on a full time basis. After dinner arrived, there was little conversation as both men sized each other up. Coffee and dessert came, and Mr. Jones gave Sam a restaurant card and wrote a name on the back, Joey Pataglia. He was told that Joey would get in touch to finalize their relationship. Sam insisted on paying for dinner since Mr. Jones would be his client and it was only apropos for Sam's company. Mr. Jones bowed to the custom. The next day Sam went to his office and waited for Joey Pataglia to call. When Pataglia called, Sam left his office, so excited, he forgot his briefcase. The only thing he did was put the receipt and card from last night's dinner in the corner of his blotter to remind to add it to the month's expenses.

CHAPTER FIVE

David is well aware of who Joey Pataglia is. It is his job to stay on top of people in the news, as that is one source of recruiting clients. Joey had made headlines several times over the last six months with his support of the mayor's reelection bid. There had been several questions and concerns over city construction contracts and, of course, Pataglia's name always surfaces as the winning bidder. Everyone knows he is well connected. The fact that Emily's missing husband is linked to this major player in the city's politics is unsettling. What could they want from him? If he is involved with Joey, what role could he play, and where is he? His background is in mostly residential real estate, so in what way would he be beneficial to the mob? Did Sam stumble onto something during his prospecting that he should not have? The only ties, if any, would be through real estate. If there is foul play, most likely his body is laying under tons of concrete in one of the city's new construction projects. Now my question is, do I get involved and help Emily? It could only lead to trouble, if in fact, her husband is connected somehow to the family. Also, it cannot bode well for Emily either way. The shock that her husband has a past or the finality of his death or never knowing what happened to him could be too overwhelming. After weighing the pros and cons, David realized that Emily intrigued him. Most women he dealt with would have moved on with their lives, realizing their husband was either dead or eloped with another woman. Besides, she was kind of attractive, to say the least. In fact, she was stunning. He wanted to get to know her better and what better way than to work together to solve a mystery. He decided that he would take the job. The odds of finding her husband alive or discovering his body at this point was a long shot. She needed help and he thought, who better to lend a hand and also make money than himself.

It was now 4:15 as David dialed Emily's number. She answered on the second ring, anticipating his call. After a polite exchange of greetings, she told him she would like to hire him. David then suggested that they meet at his office to review the information she had and to discuss a strategy moving ahead.

David's office was not what Emily had expected. It was neat, and well organized, and the furniture was old, but comfortable looking. He worked alone and did not have an answering service. In fact, there was no desk phone. He worked off his cell. A computer and printer were the only pieces of equipment he had. His license hung on the wall, along with a few commendations he had received, from his time working for the FBI as an FBI agent. Emily had Googled David and learned that he was single, never been married, was a graduate of Duke University, with a major in criminology. He has been a private investigator for ten years. It appeared that he had done a lot of traveling over the years as indicated by the amount of decorations around the office from foreign places. Some oriental, some European, with a British Flag hanging on one wall. Maybe he had a British background, although she was unable to pick up on any accent. His hair was short and neat. He had a slight tan and was actually very handsome. *Wow,* she thought. *What am I thinking? I need to concentrate on the issues at hand.* They met for over two hours going over every possible scenario. David grilled her about her home life, looking for any clue that Sam may have a hidden agenda. He questioned her about her own motives for wanting to find her husband, which made her a little uncomfortable. He wanted to make sure that Emily was totally committed to finding the answers behind Sam's disappearance. He also needed to assure himself that she wasn't involved. The only lead they had was the receipt from Labella's Italian Restaurant and the card with Joey Pataglia's name on it. Where to go from here? At 9:00 p.m. they decided to pause their conversation until tomorrow, because Emily had to get up early the following day to teach. David said he needed to check out a few things and he would call her the next day.

David's next move was to find out more about Labella's Restaurant, such as who owns it, before he starts snooping around in that area. Also, what connection does Joey Pataglia have to the restaurant? The place would seem to be out of Sam's customary places to frequent because of the upscale clientele and expensive menu. Most of Sam's clients were middle class and quite a few were first time buyers, according to his files. David needed help from a source that he did not want to use, but he had little choice since he did not have access to the kind of information he could obtain by making one phone call. Robert Stone, FBI agent in charge, and once David's boss, could provide any information he needed. The only problem was David had not spoken to Robert in years. David kept up with Robert's career since they were once very close. David had never had a case like this one that touched on the border of organized crime, so he had not needed Robert's help. David joined the FBI right out of college. Being a criminology major and a Duke graduate, the FBI recruited him very heavily. After Quantico, David was assigned to the same city and department with Robert. They grew to be good friends immediately and worked many cases together. Stone quickly rose to the top and became David's supervisor. After Robert was transferred to another city, David did not get along with his new supervisor. Many thought David was a renegade agent, who didn't follow protocols to solve cases, but his track record was impeccable. His new boss did not like David's tactics and made his life miserable. David put in for transfers, but his reputation preceded him, so he resigned. Robert was not happy that he chose to leave the FBI. He could not convince David to stay and that put a strain on their relationship. Now he needed a favor. The very source to find the best information on any connected people or crime organization was his ex-boss and friend. Whether Robert would help him remained to be seen. David always had Robert's number, no matter where he was located, on speed dial. David made the call. As expected, Robert answered on the second ring. He was always quick to act on any situation, never missing a phone call. "Well, well, what did I do to deserve a call from you after all this time?" Robert said. He must have kept David on speed dial also. "Don't tell me you are inviting me to your wedding, because I know no one could put up with you!" David laughed and said, "Well, thanks for asking, I'm doing well, thank you."

"All these years you never called, I thought it must be earth shattering news," was Robert's comment. "Actually, I need your help, I think I may have stumbled on to something that may be more up your alley. It is a case of mine and it could involve organized crime activity." Now David had Robert's attention. "Come to my office in two days. We should not discuss this over the phone," said Stone. "I'll be there, and thank you, Robert."

The next day David told Emily of his plan to meet with Robert and possibly get some answers if there is any connection between her husband, Joey Pataglia, organized crime, and who owns the Labella Italian Restaurant. He warned her not to act on her own and to stay away from the restaurant until he returned with some answers.

In their younger days, Robert and David worked on special assignment in Oxford, England, to recover a stolen manuscript. The pair made an investigative visit to the University of Oxford's Vere Harmsworth Library, which is the library's academic institution for the study and research of US history and culture. A very old and valuable manuscript was stolen from the library and the United States government sent their special investigators abroad in order to attempt to recover this important part of American cultural property. The library houses an extensive collection of sources relating to American history and a political campaigns archive. Both men were intrigued by the prospect of traveling overseas to Britain to carry out the mission. The leader of the MI5, which stands for Military Intelligence, Section 5 is Britain's domestic secret intelligence, greeted them at the headquarters at Thomas House, London. Upon arrival at the entrance of the Vere Harmsworth Library, they were escorted to the library's main desk by the head librarian, where the conservator of the special collections was sitting. Immediately, David was struck by the conservator's beauty. She was young with dark eyes and auburn hair. The librarian introduced the conservator as Mrs. Victoria Anstruther-Jones. Victoria warmly greeted them and reiterated the story of the missing manuscript. Victoria was an American, who has been the head of conservation at the library for a few years. David asked her how she wound up in England. She told him her husband was an Englishman and a professor of European history. He worked at Oxford University. Over the next few days, David worked closely with Victoria, analyzing every detail of how the manuscript was displayed and who had access to it. Stone worked with the MI5 agent on who or why someone would steal such an important artifact. One thing lead to another, and as time went on David and Victoria became infatuated with one another. When word of an affair got out, David was called back to the States. The only thing he brought back from England was their national flag to remind him of Victoria.

CHAPTER SIX

Sam could hardly contain his excitement as he drove to the meeting. He sure could use a big payday. Emily, being a teacher, did not make enough to keep up with the bills and his business is so sporadic. This country has it all wrong, he thought. We are upside down compared to other countries. Teachers, fireman, and policemen are the lowest paid professions, but yet have the largest impact on society. Sam's clients were mostly low to middle class people and first time home buyers. His referrals came from this group, mostly other family members and friends who were in the same economic position. He was grateful for this referral base, but he had to work hard to get them qualified for a mortgage. Either their credit needed to be repaired, or they lacked enough credit history. Either way, he was quite good at helping his clients to overcome most of these obstacles. Now he needed to think about preparing himself for this big meeting. *What questions will they ask? I need to make a good impression*, he thought. They were meeting at an old, vacant warehouse on the east part of town off a major highway. Easy access to the highway may have been a reason for the interest. He researched the property, but it was not listed. Maybe it's a for sale by owner, or not advertised publicly, if in fact this is the property they want to purchase. He pulled into a deserted parking lot in front of the vacant warehouse. No cars or people around. He sat in his van in front of the building and suddenly got a sick feeling in his stomach. Was this a hoax? Was I set up? He sat and waited. Finally, a black limousine pulled beside him on the passengers' side of his van. The windows were darkly tinted, preventing him from seeing inside.

After a minute, a large, bulging, middle-aged man dressed in black got out of the limo and motioned for Sam to meet him. Sam hesitated at first and thought, maybe I should have brought someone. He walked around the front of the van when the back door of the limo opened and a well-dressed man with dark, slicked down, black hair stepped out to greet Sam. He extended his hand and invited Sam to get in the back seat, never introducing himself. Sam again hesitated, but the large man was blocking his retreat. Again, the man told him to get in the limo. He obliged, but became very nervous. They pulled away onto the highway and headed north.

"Where are we going?" asked Sam.

"In good time," was the reply he got.

"What about my car?" Sam asked.

"It will be taken care of."

What does that mean? he thought. "What is this all about?"

The man in the back seat in the expensive suit replied, "You are about to receive an offer that you will not want to refuse."

Suddenly Sam felt fifty shades of black.

CHAPTER SEVEN

Emily was anxious to meet with David because he gave her hope. Her fellow teachers were very supportive and sympathetic initially, but their concern dwindled as time passed, and she only received a curious inquiry now and then. She thought about her relationship with Sam all the time when she was alone. She wished they had spent more time together. She did not know if and why they could not have a child or whose fault it was. They did not want to know. They gave up having a child a long time ago.

It was difficult to see anything through the tinted windows of the limo. Sam had no idea where they were headed. There was no conversation. Everyone just stared straight ahead. After what seemed like forever, the limo slowed down and came to a stop. The large man on the passenger's side opened his door and got out of the car. The driver did not shut off the engine. Sam did not know if it was a temporary stop or what. Just then the back doors opened, and Sam was told to step out of the limo. Sam looked around and saw a large building with two massive figures standing guard at the front door. "Follow me," the large man in black said. Sam's quick observation of the building told him it was some kind of a fortress. Square as much as he could tell with a flat roof and constructed of brick with bars on the windows. Cyclone fencing surrounded the area with barb wire. Was this an old holding jail or a prison? Once inside it all made sense. *I am going to be here for a long time*, thought Sam. Two men grabbed Sam and tied him to a chair. Chains with cuffs hung from the ceiling. He panicked. No turning back now. What did they want from him?

He had nothing of value in my business or personal assets, thought Sam. He was starting to sweat profusely. Sam felt lightheaded and dizzy. He wanted to throw up. The man who had introduced himself as Mr. Jones at the Labella Restaurant came walking toward Sam. "What do you want from me?" Sam demanded. "I have nothing of value for you."

"Quite the contrary, Mr. Carson, you possess something we value very much. You're related to the Leone family." Sam had not heard his mother's maiden name or used it in years. He had not had contact with his uncles for as long as he could remember. He remembered hearing their conversations on those Sundays when he was young. He had no idea then what those meeting of his uncles were all about and just now realized what gravity those decisions may have effected other's lives until now. Was this some sort of act of revenge against his family? What did they do? Who did they hurt during their reign of power? He guessed he was about to find out.

CHAPTER EIGHT

David arrived at Stone's office first thing in the morning. He knew Robert was an early riser and would be at the office before anyone else. He lost his wife seven years ago in an automobile accident and, since then, buried himself in his work. The guard at the front desk had to check David's ID and register him in, then check his list for verification as a visitor. After handing him a visitor pass, David was told to take the elevator to the second floor and turn right to Robert's office. Stone was already at work, going through a stack of papers. He stood up and greeted David with a long, firm handshake. He seemed to have missed David more than David realized. As is his nature, he quickly asked about the reason for David's request for information. "It's a missing case that I am working on," he explained. "What I needed to know is if you have anything in your files or any knowledge of a Joey Pataglia?" Stone just stared at David for a few brief moments. Then asked, "Where did you come across his name?"

David went on to explain the details of the case and how Pataglia was connected to the Labella Italian Restaurant. Stone was very quiet and intent, which indicated that he had hit onto something. Finally, after a long pause, Stone told David that what he was about to tell him was privileged and highly confidential information.

Emily's heart raced when she received David's call. He would be back in town the next day. She asked if the trip was beneficial? He said he would tell her in person. He didn't want to discuss what he'd found out over the phone because if there were people involved in Sam's disappearance they could have Emily's phone tapped.

They met the next afternoon after Emily's got off work. David picked her up in front of her school building and they drove to a local fast food chain and ordered a cup of coffee. Emily did not want anything to eat. She was too anxious to hear his news to eat. David had gone over in his mind a hundred times how he would relay the information that Stone gave him to Emily. How much should he tell her? Could he completely trust her to keep the information confidential? Would emotion over rule good sense?

Sam was left alone, still tied to the chair. He thought that was deliberate, in order to get his mind wrapped around the severity of his situation. Obviously, they needed something from him or he would either be dead or not here at all. After his mother passed away he had no contact with her side of the family. He knew of his uncles' exploits. Occasionally, they made the news in one fashion or another. One, a successful contractor, another, a successful insurance CEO for a major company. Still another became a high profile attorney. The rest who were still alive were minor players for one of the three successful brothers. He remembered the family being involved in a number of illegal operations. After college, he was again approached to work for the family, but he refused. He never really discussed his family history with Emily. *Whatever they wanted of me, I hope they leave her out of it*, Sam thought. Just then, Mr. Jones, if that is his real name, pulled up a chair in front of Sam. He leaned in close to Sam's face and stared into his eyes. He was sizing Sam up to see any sign of stress or weakness. Sam did his best to disguise his fears. "What's your real name?" asked Sam. "At least tell me that."

Mr. Jones looked at him and said, "That is not important. The important thing is that you listen to me very carefully. You have a cousin, the son of your uncle Frank, who has been taking over your family's drug distribution. He has been branching out and is starting to interfere with our operation. Your resemblance to him is uncanny. In fact, you could pass for him. Unfortunately, he has suffered a major accident. My interests will be blamed for his fate, if and when it is ever discovered what happened to him. There would be retribution. My major supplier would dry up at the hint of any warring between our families. We need you to go to our drug manufacturing and suppliers operation and pose as your cousin until we can complete a takeover and establish our own network. This will keep the supplier your cousin was soliciting and your family from knowing of your cousin's untimely death. They never met him, but know about him. He was trying to establish them as their new source. Your family thinks he left yesterday to procure the new line of distribution and do not expect him back for at least a week."

"How did you know about my ties to my family?" asked Sam.

"We make it our business to know everything and everybody connected to our rivals. Now let me explain to you why you will do this and what your compensation will be," said Mr. Jones.

David and Emily drank their coffee in silence. Emily was trying to digest what he had just told her. She did not know a lot about Sam's family history. He was always evasive whenever she asked him questions concerning his childhood and family members. She just figured he had some traumatic experiences in his upbringing. With her experience as a special needs teacher, she decided a long time ago to give him his space. Maybe one day he would open up and share this with her. But to find out under these conditions sent her for a loop. David told her Sam's family history, well documented from his young days when he survived under the rule of the notorious black hand. Sam's family ties go back to organized crime. David convinced her that Sam was not an active member of the organized crime family, as far as the FBI knew. However, Joey Pataglia, was a very well connected member of the organized crime family that the FBI had under their surveillance. Drugs, gambling, extortion, prostitution, racketeering, and all the regular vices associated with organized crime were tied to Pataglia. The Labella Italian Restaurant was owned by a company registered under the name Blue Sky Enterprise and a Mr. Jones, which he assumed was a false name, as the manager. Sam being a rival family member cast a new possibility of his disappearance. A family feud, revenge, blackmail, or any number of reasons raise a new question as to why Sam could have gone missing or presumed dead. Pataglia's backing the incumbent mayor, has the FBI closely monitoring the upcoming election. Once again she asked what connection Sam could have had in all this. Finally, she needed a breather from all this. She was overwhelmed and scared. She asked David to take her back to her car at the school building. She got out of David's car when he opened her door. Suddenly, she embraced him and held onto him for several minutes trying to calm herself. She was in tears. He held her tightly and wiped the tears from her eyes. Her hair had a soft flowery scent and her cheek was soft to his touch. He raised her head and kissed her firmly on the lips. She did not recoil as he hoped she wouldn't. Instead, she kissed him back with a long lingering kiss that made his head spin. He felt her warm, intense body against his and he wanted this to last forever. She wanted so badly to invite him over to her house, but reality came back and she broke their embrace. She stepped back, then leaned in and gave him a quick kiss and quickly got in her car and drove away. David stood there and watched her as she drove away. He never got involved in any other case he had like this, but this was different. It just felt right. He forgot his three rules of business; never get in a pissing contest with a skunk, never try to make chicken salad out of chicken shit, and lastly, as the rule he just broke, never shit where you eat, which means you never sleep with the client.

Sam was furnished with a new ID to match his cousin. He was outfitted with a whole new wardrobe and schooled on all the intricacies of the drug trafficking world. He was drummed with all the names of the major players he needed to know. He was refamiliarized with his family and their operations. He was trained on how to conduct himself as to not raise any suspicions. His sole purpose was to get in and out as quickly as possible and pull off posing as his cousin, leaving the drug suppliers believing that Sam, as Carmen, represented his family, thus buying valuable time for Mr. Jones and his organization. He had no idea where he was going. He was a nervous wreck. If he failed, he may never return home. If they found out he was an impostor, they would surely kill him. If he did not go through with the plan, the consequences would be even worse. What would his family think? *Will I be viewed as a traitor? I'm in a no win situation no matter what. The only thing I can hope for was to come out of this with the least the amount of damage. What's going to happen to Emily? I may never see her again,* thought Sam. She would be all alone.

No children. No family of her own. Her parents had since passed away. Her father was an alcoholic. Her mother died of breast cancer and she did not have any siblings. With her personality and attractiveness, she should have no trouble finding someone and having another chance to be happy. Now he needed to concentrate on the mission so to speak. For his survival, he had to be confident and well versed on the operation at hand. He was not told what happened to his cousin. He was scared to ask. No matter what happens, when the truth comes out, all hell will break loose. Whether Sam will be here to see it remains to be seen.

CHAPTER NINE

Emily was beside herself. What had she done? Evan though her husband had been missing, she was still legally married. Was this an excuse to behave this way? She could not deny the feelings she is getting for David. After all these months, she is very lonely, not to mention his good looks and charm. Was she just looking for someone to lean on? *No*, she thought, *he is more than that. Is he just filling the void left by Sam's disappearance? No once again.* The chemistry is growing between them, she realized. She also was aware of some snide remarks by a few of her fellow teachers concerning the amount of time she is spending with David. They did not realize the relationship her and David had. They had to work closely to be able to maximize the effort to find Sam. At least that's what she is telling herself.

David spent the night going over his information from Stone. He now knew of Sam's background and his families' ties to organized crime. But where did Sam fit into the picture? His thoughts kept getting interrupted with what happened between Emily and him. He needed to concentrate on the issues at hand, but could not get her out of his mind. What if they did find Sam? Then what would happen between them? Once, he was involved with another man's wife on a case, but he swore he would never do that again. He put aside his notes and poured a glass of red wine. His affair with Victoria was pure lust. He was younger, away from home, and a new agent for the FBI. It was one of his first cases and he and Stone were sent to England for a collaboration case with the MI5. He was charmed and seduced by her beauty. Her husband was a stuffy, prudish, professor at Oxford University, who believed a relationship should be properly conducted as English society dictated. He somehow, along the way, forgot or lost interest to the fact he was married to an American beauty. Victoria was a free spirit and needed more than a proper relationship. They immediately bonded. She found him sexually attractive and able to satisfy her deepest desires. Their relationship was brief, but memorable. They both knew it would go nowhere, so they enjoyed the time they had together. Emily was another matter. It was more than a sexual attraction. He felt a deep connection with her. Her infectious personality, along with her girlish humor and innocence, even in a time of despair, were remarkable. The other cases he had involved high maintenance, self-centered, egotistical women. He could have had various relationships with many of them over the years, but they were mostly a turn off. All they cared about was the inconvenience they were going through to move on with their lives. On one hand, his respect for his professionalism dictated for him to solve the case and move on. On the other hand, he secretly was hoping her husband would never surface. The problem would be, could she move on never knowing what happened to Sam?

Sam was driven to the airport in the black limo. He was headed to an unknown location in Mexico. That's all he knew. He was told he would be met when he landed. His destination from there was a mystery. Usually drug cartels liked to keep manufacturing and distribution sites unknown. Sam was getting very nervous and could not relax during the flight. He hoped he had absorbed enough information to pull off the masquerade. His new name was Carmen Leone, his cousin's name, who is also Sam's age. He has not seen Carmen or spoken to him since their college days. They went their separate ways after Carmen could not convince Sam to join the family operation. Carmen was a business major, the same as Sam, but they attended different colleges. Carmen went away to school, but Sam stayed home in order to work to pay for his education. Now he thought that might not have been the best decision to refuse the families' help. As he departed the plane, he was immediately met by three well-dressed Hispanic men. They led him to a black Escalade parked on the tarmac. Before he got into the car, they asked for his identification and frisked him. He sat in the back with one of the men. They did not speak to Sam as they drove out of a back gate on the landing strip. The windows were tinted, so it was hard to see much of the landscape. After a period of time, they turned onto a dusty road. They continued for several miles and pulled into a dirt lot with a large fenced in building. "Honey, I'm home," from the movie *The Shining*, came to Sam's mind. He was about to enter crazy land.

David called Stone to see if he had thought of any other information he could share with him. When they finished their previous meeting, Stone said he had one more source he wanted to check. "Let me call you back on a secure line," he said.

Ten minutes later, Stone called. His source told him that Joey Patalia was connected to one of the biggest cartels out of Mexico. The FBI was working close with the Drug Enforcement Agency, monitoring any major moves in process. As far as Mr. Jones goes, they believe he is the major contact person in the organization who Pataglia reports to and is responsible for the ties to the Mexican cartel. They did get wind of the Leone family trying to make a move to secure the cartel operation's services, which could have some major fall out between the families. Sam Carson's name never came up in any discussions with the DEA. Stone thinks he is clean, but could be a silent player in reserve when the family needs his services. David hoped for Sam's sake that he was not involved, because that could be the reason he is missing. Involvement and disappearance usually tie together.

Emily found it hard to concentrate on her students. She was thinking that maybe she needed a leave of absence. Fifteen highly autistic kids are very demanding and deserve her full attention. She was always praised that she went over and above her duties as a teacher because she developed the whole child. Now she thought she was not capable of putting forth the effort to accomplish this goal. The months of questioning and doubting had drained her. She felt she does not even know who her husband is. Her interest in David was starting to cloud her thinking. How much longer can she retain his services? We could be stepping into some dangerous situations as indicated by detective Becket and Stone's information. *How much at this point do I really want to know? I'm sure David is not telling me everything. What is he holding back?* she thought. David was to call her that after noon in order to discuss their next play. That thought kept her going on this day.

CHAPTER TEN

Sam got out of the car and was escorted into the building. From the outside, he could not tell how big the building was. It was built like a large warehouse, with separate sections on both sides with a long, wide hallway going down the center. Each room along the sides had two armed guards at the door ways. A conveyer belt extended from one end to the other. There was an open upper level walkway with a guard rail running around the entire building with heavily armed guards stationed every twenty feet apart. Sam wasn't sure, but his best guess was that at least a hundred people were in the building. Some of the sectioned off rooms had no ceilings. Stacks of wooden pallets were lined up neatly in each corner. Large air vents were placed over each room. Most of the people he saw were dressed in white outfits similar to hospital scrubs and they wore masks. They also wore gloves. This obviously was a manufacturing facility. Cocaine was his guess. He was led to a large, well decorated office in the back corner of the building. A short heavy set man stood up and greeted him with a warm handshake. "Welcome, Mr. Leone, I trust your trip was pleasant. My name is Carlos." He motioned for him to have a seat across from his desk. The two men who escorted him stepped back to close the door and stood next to it. Carlos offered Sam a refreshment. Carlos explained that he was the operating manager of the building. He apologized for the secrecy of the location, but trusted that Sam would understand. Carlos said he was given instructions that he was to meet with Sam and to give him a tour and explain the distribution process as a possible new purchaser of their product. Carlos said his boss had met with Sam's family and arranged for this meeting. Sam wanted to ask his boss's name, but thought that might raise suspicion. "We produce hundreds of pounds of cocaine a week," Carlos said. He also told Sam that most large dealers have no concept of what or how cocaine is manufactured and processed, and don't care. "Cocaine is a high-priced way of getting high, which is why they are in this business. It has a certain mystique. It's referred to as the caviar of street drugs. Cocaine is seen as the status heavy drug of celebrities, fashion models, and Wall Street traders. That's what makes it such a lucrative business."

As Sam got the tour of the facility, Carlos explained that cocaine is a pure extract from the coca bush that grows in the Andres region of South America. "There are two types of cocaine. Powdered cocaine, commonly known on the street as coke or blow. The other is crack cocaine, commonly known as crack or rock, which we leave for the black dealers to process," Carlos said. He informed Sam that cocaine is known by a variety of names, such as coke, Charlie, C, Pepsi, nose candy, and is the most commonly used recreational drug, "Which is great for business," he said with a laugh. Sam could not see in every room and only went into a few. He didn't' need to. He saw enough. For what he was exposed to now, he would be killed immediately if they knew the reason he was here. Carlos told him that there were many distributions methods. His favorite was in dead animals. Another was a coffin, with drugs planted inside the corpse. Sam wandered, where did they get the dead bodies? He didn't want to know. One of them could be his. Hidden on trucks, among a big load, were the most common methods. Lumber shipments and private air planes, were reliable ways for trafficking. Carlos said that their US connection would tie in his families' receiving places. The price, amounts, and shipment frequency will be negotiated by their bosses. "We are always looking to expand. I know you must be tired after a long day. My drivers will take you to your hotel, and I will pick you up for dinner later. We have some other things to discuss and people to meet. If the negotiations go well, I understand you will be our contact and representative for your family on all our dealings.

In fact, you are to remain here until everything is settled and finalized," Carlos said.

Just then, Sam's heart sank. He was in a catch-22. If the negotiations did not go well, there was no way that the cartel would just let him leave. He knew and saw too much. If a deal, in fact, worked out and agreed to, then he would eventually be exposed as an imposter to the cartel and a traitor to his family. He was trapped. He did not know which fate would be worse. He had no way out of this situation. They took his cell phone because of the secrecy of the location, so no one could trace him or track his location. Who would he call anyway? The only ones he could call had sent him here on a suicide mission. They would be glad to know he was being held, which would buy them more time to implement their plan for a takeover. This is exactly why they sent him in the first place. How long could he remain alive here? Did Mr. Jones have another Mexican connection to take over this cocaine operation? He knew it was only a matter of time until his family discovered that Carmen was either missing or dead. What if they called to talk to whom they thought was Carmen? Now it hit Sam. Carmen was not sent here to represent the Leone family. He was part of the bargaining chip. He was sent as the sacrificial lamb, for ransom, to show the good faith and intent to the cartel. Obviously, Mr. Jones knew this, and wanted his own man inside. If anything happened to Sam as Carmen, then the Leone family would hold the cartel responsible. This would be a major coup for Mr. Jones. He knew Sam was a dead man either way. When the family found out about my deception, and demise, the cartel would ultimately be blamed for Carmen also.

David thought, who is this mystery man, Mr. Jones? He may be the clue or missing piece to this puzzle. He knows Patalgia works for him, so he must be pretty high on the family pecking order. From his knowledge, organized crime families have an intricate infrastructure. One boss, controls the family and is the ultimate authority within the organization and makes all the major decisions involving the criminal group. An under boss insulates the boss from potential criminal prosecution. They also translate the boss's orders to the lower ranking members. There is also a counselor, or adviser, who could be a high profile attorney for the organization. He advises the boss on the intricacies of criminal activities and provides unbiased advice on how to handle matters within the family and matters concerning the law. The next level is a captain. They are the street bosses who run the day to day operations of the organization. They receive their orders from either the boss or under boss. Which one is Mr. Jones, and which one is Mr. Pataglia? What did Jones or Pataglia want from Sam?

CHAPTER ELEVEN

Emily met David at the local park. People were already starting to talk about them, so she did not want to be around the school. He was waiting for her on a park bench. He stood up to greet her and awkwardly extended his hand. She took it and held it for a brief moment. They sat down and exchanged pleasantries. She asked if he had any new developments and if he figured out who this Pataglia is. He told her that he is somehow connected to a large organized crime family. Not Sam's family, that much he knew. He is either an under boss or a so called captain for the organization. That would place him as a very dangerous man. She stood up and asked if they could go for a walk. She told him she was thinking of taking a leave of absence from her school. She needed to distance herself from the whole situation. David asked if that meant from him also? She thought, *Hell no, I want you to go with me*, but she was hesitant to suggest such an idea.

"Look," he said, "why don't we go and visit Robert Stone and let you meet him. He has been very helpful. It's a short drive and we could stay for a day or two and enjoy the break."

"What about your other cases?" she asked.

"They can wait. There is nothing urgent, that can't wait." Wow she thought, this is a big step. Am I ready for this? Then she thought, *Why not? This is a business trip. I need a break away after all these months*. Emily had over forty five sick and personal days saved up. She and Sam hadn't had a vacation in years. She taught summer school every year so this left little time for them. She wasn't sure if this was her safety net for not wanting to go away with Sam during the summers, or because Sam always said that summer was his best months for selling houses and hated to leave during this busy time of the year. Emily relented and accepted David's offer. She called her principal and the company that assigns substitutes for her classroom.

Sam was in his heavily guarded hotel room when the phone rang. It was the voice of Carlos's driver. He said to come down to the lobby in ten minutes. Dress was casual. Sam got on the elevator with his two armed guards. They met Carlos's driver who lead them to a black sedan. Carlos was sitting in the back seat. He motioned for Sam to get in the car. Sam sat between Carlos and one of the bodyguards. "How are your accommodations?" he was asked.

"Great," was Sam's reply. A last luxury before my sentence to death, thought Sam. Carlos said they were headed to one of his favorite night spots, where they would have food, liquor, and some of the best looking women in all of Mexico. *Again*, Sam thought, *my last meal.* The club was large with several floors. From what he could see, from the sign at the entrance, there was different entertainment on each floor. The main dining room was on the main floor and had a seating area for at least two hundred people. This made the Labella Italian Restaurant look small in comparison. They sat at a table on the back wall. The two bodyguards stood beside Carlos, leaning against the wall. Sam sat across from Carlos. A waiter came to the table with a chilled bottle of champagne. Carlos had ordered ahead of time. He toasted the deal and the waiter handed the menus. Carlos said they have the best steaks this side of Texas. Pure bred beef from a ranch nearby that they receive fresh every day. As far as Mexican food, Carlos said he never touches it. "Too fattening. Not good for your health and figure," said the small, much over weight man. At least he has a sense of humor. They ordered two twelve ounce stakes, medium, mashed potatoes with brown gravy, and a large salad, with Italian dressing. How Ironic.

David picked up Emily early the next morning. He called Stone last night after leaving Emily and set up a lunch date for the next afternoon. Stone did not think it was such a good idea, because he had little to add to the situation without divulging compromising, classified information. She could be a loose cannon and it could undermine the already ongoing investigation. He had no idea why David was doing this except to keep his case going in hopes of a break through, or just milking the situation. The latter did not seem like something David would do. He has always perceived David as a professional with ethics. Oh well, he figured, he would find out at lunch.

Emily was dressed in tight, form-fitting designer jeans that showed off her lean figure. She wore a loose blue pullover jersey which accentuated her beautiful blue eyes. He opened the car door for her, which she thought was very charming. It had been a long time since she was shown such courtesy. As they headed out, he told her what to expect from Stone. He was usually all business, but doubted that he would be forthcoming on any new information. The weather was very pleasant and mild. A great day to take off and get away. He could feel Emily start to relax. This is good for her. She needed a diversion from all the stress of Sam and her classroom.

Stone arrived at the restaurant early and was sipping his water when David walked in with who he thought was Emily. Now Stone knew why David was putting so much effort into this case. She was stunning. She was casual yet elegant. Her blonde hair and striking blue eyes were mesmerizing. He hoped David was not putting himself in a situation similar to the England fiasco. That was a long time ago and hopefully David had matured enough to avoid those encounters. Stone stood and greeted them with a handshake. Emily took one glance at Stone to know David was right on about Stone's personality. He was tall and rugged looking in a handsome way. He definitely fit her mental picture of a FBI Director. No one to mess with and all business. David and Stone probably made a formidable pair working together. Stone expressed his condolence on her husband's disappearance. He asked her about her career as a teacher, never understanding why anyone would go into that under paid, nonappreciative profession. As their conversations continued, Stone began to understand that she was pursuing her calling. If he had a child, he would want her to be their teacher. He could also see how great she is with special needs children. It seems unfortunate that good people like her, who make such a large contribution to society, suffer more than most. He sees this all the time in his occupation. He wishes he could find more answers for her. When lunch was over, Stone looked at his watch and said he had to excuse himself. He had a staff meeting scheduled for this afternoon. "It was a pleasure meeting you Emily. I hope you find the answers you are looking for." Stone asked for the check and left. "Well, what did you think?" David asked.

"He was just how you described him," said Emily.

They left the restaurant and went to the local mall. It had been a long time since Emily did any shopping for herself. She wanted to check out the women's stores. David had no problem accompanying her. He had never been on a shopping trip with a woman. He dated his share of women, but was never in a close relationship. Never married, engaged, or even close. He thought this would be entertaining. Emily was like a little girl in a candy store. He sat patiently while she tried on pants and dresses from the clearance racks. He smiled as she looked for sale items, realizing she existed on a teacher's pay. Staying within her budget just made her more appealing as the no frills, plain and natural beauty she is. She could look good in clothes from the good will Dumpster. After several hours of shopping they decided to plan for dinner. They went to a local pizza shop and had pizza and beer and talked about their younger days and their colleges. She realized she knew nothing about David's past other than he worked for the FBI. David told her where he was born and raised. His dad was a tyrant and by today's laws and standards he would be locked up and the key thrown away. He was a mechanic who could repair any type of machine. "His hobby was boxing and he used me and my mother as his sparing partners and punching bag. He was a heavy smoker and eventually developed emphysema. He died of pulmonary arrest. My mother never stood up to his abuse, and I lost respect for her along the way, because she did nothing to protect me from his violence. She passed away years later of old age," David explained. He made good grades throughout school because of his father's threats. "He insisted that I make all As so he could brag to his friends. It was the only good thing he ever did for me, but I doubt that he did it for my benefit," said David. Emily shared her childhood, telling him about her alcoholic father who came home drunk every night and destroyed their dinners by turning over the table in anger. Her mother and father fought constantly. They would burn each other with cigarettes and he would punch holes in the walls. How did she turn out so sweet? That was the only word he could think of to describe her personality. In his experiences, usually the child of a dysfunctional family with a drinking problem, becomes one themselves. She was just the opposite. How fortunate for Sam to have found her first. Did he truly appreciate her? If he did lead a secret life and was tied into his families' business, he hoped he would never be found.

They checked into a hotel just off the highway for the night. They got separate rooms as David suspected she would want. After they got settled into their rooms, they met at the hotel lounge. It was getting late, but they had no reason to get up early. After all, this was a little get away from her routine. She was up every day at 5:00 a.m. for school. They sipped on glasses of red wine and by her second glass, she was starting to feel a buzz and an increase of desire to grab David and take him to her room. She stopped dead in her thoughts and realized she did not want David to think she was easy and would do anything when plied with alcohol. She finished her wine and suggested that she turn in after such an adventurous day. David walked her to her room and started to say good night, when she grabbed him and passionately kissed him. He swooned and did not want to let her go. She abruptly broke their embrace and went into her room and closed the door. David stood there for several seconds stunned. He wanted to knock on her door and invite himself in, but thought better of it. He did not want to push too hard and take the chance of driving her away. He went back to his room, hoping her kiss was in earnest and not just a thank you.

CHAPTER TWELVE

After dinner, Carlos quizzed Sam about his family's operations. Carlo asked, "How many dealers did he have contact with and how big was their territory? How many politicians did they have in their pockets? The cartel is always looking for needed protection on both sides of the border." Sam tried to bluff his way through what he perceived as an informal interrogation. Carlos could see that Sam was getting very uncomfortable with his questioning. He then suggested that they take advantage of the entertainment the club offered. Carlos motioned to one of the managers and two beautiful women came over to their table and smiled at Sam. "They're both yours," he said to Sam. A fancy hotel, a great dinner, and now two lovely women, thought Sam. I'm being sent off in style." Sam debated whether to decline, which could be an insult, but what did he have to lose. On the other hand this could be his last days and he could go out with a bang, no pun intended. It only took him a few seconds to decide.

Angelo Bartello, a.k.a. Mr. Jones, sat at his desk in the office of the organization's club. He is the boss of one of the oldest organized crime families in the city. Most of the organization was now legitimate. However, since the economic downturn, a few years back, the organization has suffered some heavy losses. So much for legitimacy, he thought. The famous bail out by our free world leader did nothing to help many business interests. It only made the banks healthy. Recovery has been slow, but the main source of income has been the drug business. When things go bad, you can always count on the population to find money for liquor and drugs. He held onto some of the old vices as a hedge against recessions and inflation. Without the drug sales, they would have serious income problems. Now he was hearing of another families' interest in his main source of supply. He could not afford any strong competition now. He held the largest share of the drug market and he was not going to relinquish any of his territory. If his supplier decided to do business with another family in this city, it would cause serious consequences. He had to be proactive. The organization counted on the boss for their income and livelihood. He was responsible for many disappearances and he did not want to be responsible for his own. He needed to nix any actions that would jeopardize their market position. He needed to devise a plan. He placed a call to Joey Pataglia, his right-hand man, to set up a meeting to strategize in order to prevent any harmful fallout.

The next morning Emily and David met for breakfast in the hotel restaurant. She had been exhausted the night before, but could hardly sleep. She wanted so badly to pull David into her room. She hasn't felt like this in years. They hardly spoke as they ate, only looking at each other occasionally and avoiding any sustained eye contact. Finally, David broke the uncomfortable silence. "What do you want to do today?"

She responded, "What would you like to do?"

David thought, *I would like to take you to a room and make mad passionate love.* He caught himself. He said maybe they should head back. She agreed. She was tired and wanted to take more time to sort out things. They left the hotel and headed home.

Joey Pataglia walked into the club and was greeted by everyone like a celebrity. He was always dressed in a shark skinned suit and a Brooks Brothers shirt with a silk tie. His shoes always had a glossy glow and he wore several diamond rings. He was not married at the present, but the next wife would be his fifth. He went straight to the office where Angelo Bartello was waiting. He leaned over the desk and shook Angelo's hand, then sat down in a chair in front of the desk. Angelo sounded irritated over the phone. He knew this meeting must be urgent. We don't usually meet face-to-face unless it's a delicate matter, involving something highly confidential. He was right. It was a very secretive meeting to formalize a plan that could lead to a major disaster if it failed. It had the ramifications of an all-out war with another family. Joey knew the financial state of the organization and knew how important it was to keep the drug trafficking end of their operation going. Angelo had come up with a masterful plan to prevent any other family from taking over their drug market. He needed Joey to orchestrate the finer details. Joey had already made contact and was building a relationship with a rival cartel. Angelo's plan was to help this cartel take over the entire operation of his present supplier. In return, his family would become their biggest buyer and distributer. His family would oversee the entire city's drug activity. He would help the cartel open new markets in other cities with his contacts. He would supply the cartel with all the inside information they needed for a takeover. All he wanted in return was their loyalty against any other families. His plan was simple. When he heard that the Leone family was pursuing his supplier, he had to act. He knew from an inside source, that the Leones had made contact with his supplier. They were sending a representative to establish a relationship and to tour their production and distribution facilities. Angelo did not want it to get that far. When he found out they were sending Carmen Leone, Frank's Leone's nephew, he had him abducted the day he was to leave so no one would miss him. The ingenious part, or stroke of luck, was that Angelo had seen Sam's property advertisements in the paper. He was a dead ringer for Carmen. Through his contacts, he had the whole history of Sam Carson and his family ties to the Leones. He knew the kid was clean, which was all the better for his plan. He would kidnap Sam and send him down to Mexico as the Leone family representative. They had all Carmen's identifications and his itinerary for the trip to Mexico. Sam would be buying valuable time for his new business partners to eliminate their competition and seize the building and equipment. When the present supplier finds out that Sam is an imposter, they will blame the Leone family for him being there. When the Leone family finds out Carmen is missing, they will blame the cartel. When the blood bath ends, the new cartel will move in and take over the operation and Angelo has eliminated his competition. Joey grabs Sam. Angelo, as Mr. Jones, makes Sam a willing player. The Leone family thinks Carmen is in Mexico and the new cartel is waiting to act. The plan was put into play.

Sam was awoken the next morning by a phone call. He was told to come down to the lobby in thirty minutes. He had a tremendous headache. He remembered leaving the club around 3:00 a.m. It was now 10:30 a.m. He left the dinner table with the two women. They lead him to a lounge area on the second floor where they started drinking shots of tequila with beer chasers. The women were young and beautiful. They laughed and smiled all night. They were there to make sure he was entertained and watched. He did not see Carlos after dinner. He was told to come down to the lobby in thirty minutes. He showered and dressed and stopped at the front desk to pour a cup of coffee. What was in store for today? He did not want to spend another day at the manufacturing building. It gave him a bad headache yesterday, with all the chemical smells. He was wondering what Mr. Jones was doing, planning an all-out assault on the building? Sam is just a pawn in this game. When would he be taken out of the game? He missed Emily so much it hurt. He longed just to talk to her and hear her voice. The two guards met him and escorted him to the car. The black limo was there, but no Carlos.

CHAPTER THIRTEEN

It was late Friday afternoon when Emily and David pulled in front of her house. She had the weekend to rest. They'd talked very little on the drive home. Emily was struggling with her emotions and David was trying to conceal his feelings.

The next day, Emily went back to Sam's office. Everything was still the way he had left it over five months ago. He owned the office condo building, so no one had access except her. She sat in his desk chair, trying to feel his presence, or any connection to him. This was his life. He had become so engrossed and preoccupied with his business that they started to drift apart several years ago. He was building his business and she had been working on another special education degree. Their relationship had become complacent. She never realized how much it had until she met David and began what started as a working relationship. She knew that Sam may never be back. After all this time, he was either dead or found someone else and entered into a new life. She had to wait at least another year or more before he could be declared officially dead. Sam has a large life insurance policy that would not payout until he was legally declared dead. The money was not important to her, in fact she did not even think about it until she was thoroughly questioned as a suspect in his disappearance. The police put her through a series of interrogations, until they realized if she had planned foul play, she would have let his body be discovered so she could claim the insurance money. Sitting in the office only made her feel lonelier. It was Saturday afternoon. She hoped to hear from David.

Three days had passed and no word from Carmen. Frank Leone knew that the cartel was secretive about their location, but he had expected a phone call. His talks with Javier Cortez, the cartel leader had gone well. Carmen was sent to show good faith on the families' part, establish a rapport, and become familiarized with how the supplier ships the cocaine to the drop off destinations. Also, to set up new routes for pickup for the families' dealers. No one in the family actually sold the drugs. They had a string of small-time dealers all over their market to do this. The family was highly insulated from direct association with drugs and used outside contacts to sell and collect the revenue. Some of the most highly respected politicians were steady customers. Frank needed to have access to larger amounts of cocaine in order to satisfy and expand the families market. He placed a call to Cortez to see if he could check on Carmen. Frank did not realize that no calls would come from Carmen that could identify the cartel's location.

Sam got in the limo and was driven in the opposite direction of the manufacturing plant. He was grateful for that. They drove for several miles then turned off onto a field. Were they taking him to where they grow the coca plants? He remembered that Carlos said that they received the leaves from South America. Then a sudden fear came over him. Was this where he was to be executed. Had he served his purpose? Did they discover his masquerade? The limo stopped in the middle of the field and he was told to get out of the car. One of the bodyguards reached in his jacket and Sam thought, this was the end. The guard pulled out a cell phone and handed it to Sam. "Call your boss," Sam was told.

David wanted to call Emily. He sat at his desk and tried to occupy his time reviewing his other cases. He just could not concentrate. His thoughts were filled with Emily. Finally he picked up the phone and called her. She answered on the second ring. He told her he just wanted to touch base. He said he was thinking of going to the Labella Italian Restaurant for dinner out of curiosity and asked if she would like to join him? He had never been there and he doubted that anyone would know them, but if they did, it could trigger a reaction that would connect some dots. It could be risky, but they have nothing else. She said she would love to go. He would pick her up at eight.

Joey Pataglia had Carmen safely tucked away at one of the families' safe houses. They kept him alive in case they had to use him for a bargaining chip. Carmen was drugged and was totally confused. "Why am I not dead," he thought? He was taken at gun point and shoved into the back seat of a car. He had no idea where he is or how long he has been held captive. He wondered if this was some kind of revenge or ransom. The only thing he could remember was getting ready to go to the airport when he left his house. *Surely my family would be looking for me. They knew who I am. They have my ID. The question is, do they know I am a member of the Leone family?* Carmen thought.

David picked up Emily at eight sharp. She greeted him at the door dressed in a black, knee length, evening dress, which accentuated her blonde hair and blue eyes. She was a knock out. They certainly will not go unnoticed at the restaurant. They were quiet as they drove the fifteen miles into town. As they parked in the lot next to the restaurant, he told her how elegant she looked. She thanked him for the compliment, but said he was just being kind. She did not see herself as elegant, but as a plain, simple girl. As they entered the restaurant, every head turned to look at them. So much for trying not to be noticed. She did look quite stunning. Every woman was jealous, and every man envious. They were seated at a small table near the back of the restaurant. The waiter complimented Emily on her beauty and asked for their drink orders. They ordered red wine and breaded cheese sticks for an appetizer. The place was elegant. The motif was Italian, as expected, with columns and paintings of the old country. Lot of vines and ornamentations adorned the entire dining area. The bar was off to one side with a whole wall of racks filled with imported wines. The place was full. The menu was very expensive and contained only Italian entrees. They both ordered the veal parmesan. David scanned the room to see if they were drawing any particular or unusual interest. He noticed a gentleman at the bar who occasionally glanced their way. He was well dressed and could have been the manager. Jake Malzone spotted Emily as soon as she walked in the restaurant. He knew she was Sam's wife. They make it their business to know family members of their victims. They had been watching her to make sure they knew her every move. She might come in handy if Sam had not cooperated. Since he did they left her alone. They also wanted to make sure Emily never found out about Sam's disappearance.

Sam took the phone. He was told to call his father, Frank. Sam did not have any idea what his uncle Frank's number was. "I'm a dead man," Sam imagined. He had to think quickly. He explained that Frank only worked from a cell phone and consistently changed his number to avoid detection or traces."

"Frank changed his number," Sam said, "just before I left for Mexico and did not give it to me. They were to communicate only when he got back." The guard grabbed the phone and looked at Sam suspiciously. They got back in the limo and headed back to the hotel.

The guard called Carlos to inform him that the phone call did not take place. When Sam walked into his room, Carlos was sitting on the couch. He did not look happy. He motioned for Sam to sit next to him. He put his arm around Sam. "Who are you and who sent you? Why are you here?" The two guards stood behind Sam. He did not know what to say.

"I've been in this business too many years and know when something does not fit. You do not fit. You haven't asked the right questions and are too nervous. I know a rat when I smell one. What I want to know is who sent you?" Carlos questioned. Sam was silent. "Either you're a narc or a spy. We'll find out," Carlos said. Sam was struck in the head from behind. He went out like a light.

Carlos could not get any information from Sam. Sam's fear of whoever he works for must have been more of a threat then Carlos. With what he had seen and now knows, they could never let him leave alive. They interrogated him for two days. He never gave it up. Whatever Mr. Jones told Sam he would do to him to make him cooperate in this escapade, must have been devastating. Carlos called his DEA inside contact who was on his payroll. He told him to find out everything he could about Carmen Leone. The snitch called back the next day and gave him Carmen's whole background. He told

Carlos that Carmen was a very informed member of the Leone family, being the son of the organization's boss. He was also an enforcer on very personal matters. He was very flashy and outgoing. He was also feared within the ranks for his violent temper. This did not fit the man who claimed to be Carmen. What was Frank Leone up to sending this imposter? Was he negotiating in bad faith by not wanting to put his son in harm's way if their deal went south? Now he had no reason to trust Leone. I should send his messenger boy back to him in pieces. He now was sure that Sam was an imposter. He decided to keep Sam alive for a little while longer in case he needed him for leverage. Carlos called Cortez and explained the new development.

CHAPTER FOURTEEN

David and Emily enjoyed the dinner. It had been a long time since she dressed up to go out. She felt special this evening. David kept admiring her all night. He complimented her dress. He told her how nice she looked. He made sure he never mentioned Sam. He wanted this night for himself and wanted Emily's full attention. She was absolutely captivating. After a glass of wine she was glowing. He reached over and held her hand and thanked her for making this evening so special. She blushed and thanked him. She was living in the moment. His charming and calm personality were really getting to her. She needed to feel like a woman again, it's been a long time. Neither wanted the night to end. When David asked for the check, she excused herself to go to the ladies room. She looked in the mirror. She quickly analyzed her life. Sam was a good man, but he had not been very passionate. Maybe married for ten years will do that to a man. David, on the other hand, seemed very passionate. He was easy to talk to, a gentleman in every way, very concerned about her feelings, a good listener, and quite handsome. She wanted to take him home with her, but in good conscience, she could not take that final step till she knew the fate of her husband.

Sam was a prisoner in a small room in who knows where. His head was still ringing from the blow from behind. He went through an excruciating and painful interrogation at the hands of one of Carlos's henchmen. He was tied to a chair and was deprived of sleep. He hadn't eaten or drank anything since he was taken. Occasionally, during questioning, one of the guards would hold a phone book to his side, and another guard would hit the book with a baseball bat whenever they did not like his answers. The blows temporarily took away his breath. He was gasping for air. He was getting weak. He could feel the strength oozing from his body. No food, no water, and no sleep will do this to a man. The only thought he held onto was the threat Mr. Jones made of Emily being raped repeatedly, every bone in her body broken, and then skinned alive. He now realized that there was no compensation for him. He was on a one way trip. When Jones told him that he would be compensated for his help or suffer the consequences if he refused to cooperate, the consequence was the only thing Jones meant to carry out. How long could he hold out? Carlos was running out of patience. They stepped up their method to get Sam to talk. While he was strapped to the chair so he could not move, a bucket of water was suspended over his head. Cold water slowly dripped onto his forehead. The forehead was found to be the most suitable point because of its sensitivity. He could see each drop coming and after long duration it gradually would drive him frantic. The psychological effect would drive him mad and ultimately break him. The guards left him to this slow torture and hoped this would make him more cooperative.

Frank called Cortez for some answers. Cortez was not very forthcoming concerning Sam's, who Frank thought was Carmen, status. Cortez needed to buy time for Carlos to sort things out, so he told him he would look into it. Cortez did not trust Leone, but needed to find out what if he was up to something. Their deal seemed legit in the beginning, but now it took on a new twist. An imposter representing the Leone family? This was a breach of trust. Why would Frank do this and be so concerned about someone who was not his son? Competition among cartels was always fierce. Was Frank setting his cartel up for a takeover? There has been talk about a cartel trying to muscle in on his market. He did not know who they were or who the cartel leader was yet, but through Carlos's interrogation of the imposter, he hoped to find out and overt any action against his cartel. He called Angelo Bartello to see if he could shed any light on this new cartel operation or if he has been approached about doing business with them.

Bartello got the call he wanted, which was a nervous and upset Cortez. He told Cortez he heard of a possible cartel take over, but he had never been approached by anyone soliciting his business. He said he was informed that the Leone family was reaching out to expand their drug territory. He did his best to convince Cortez by implicating the Leone family as much as he could to make them appear deceitful. He added that another group was entertaining them and were vying for their drug business. "The cartel was a new one out of Columbia," said Bartello, "and were trying to establish themselves in my city, which would affect our distribution and sales. Maybe the Leone family is trying to secure the whole market, which would leave us both at a loss. If the Leones are dealing with them, maybe they are helping this new cartel by securing inside information on your operation. Do you know of any serious activity within your operation?" Dead silence. Bartello now knew his plan was working. Cortez was starting to put the pieces together.

Talk on the street and chatter monitored by the FBI had rumored that Carmen, crime boss Frank Leone's son, had disappeared months before David sought him out for information on Joey Pataglia. Robert Stone did not tell David because he thought it had nothing to do with the disappearance case he was working. After checking out Carson's background, he wasn't so sure that Sam Carson's and Carmen Leone's disappearances weren't somehow connected. They went missing about the same time. They were cousins. Frank Leone, reputed crime boss of the Leone family, was Sam's uncle. Quite a coincidence, both from the same family. Maybe Kimbro was on to something. Neither one has surfaced. His contact in the DEA told him months ago that there was warring among cartels for the cocaine distribution business. Some heavy hitters in the drug business were replaced with a renegade cartel from Columbia. They were rumored to have the support of the Bartello family. The cartel leader traveled under fictitious names and the DEA never could identify him. The Mexican police reported several fresh grave pits they discovered in a field in a remote part of Mexico. The bodies were too mutilated for recognition. They couldn't tell if Sam or Carmen were among them.

He didn't know if he should tell David about the possible connection or not, but he didn't want David unprepared for any backlash.

Cortez called Carlos immediately after he hung up with Leone and asked if he had any information from the imposter. For now he kept the information he found out and put together to himself until it could be verified by their prisoner. "Do what you have to do to obtain any information from their captive," he told Carlos. "Keep him alive for now." Cortez felt very vulnerable. He could be attacked from two fronts. The Leone family and the new cartel were threatening his livelihood and mere existence.

Carlos walked into the cold, damp room where Sam was tied to a chair with the overhead drip still hitting his forehead with a rhythmic flow. He looked into Sam's eyes. They just stared back at him with a blank look. The torture had pushed him over the brink. Carlos slapped him on the cheek and there was no reaction. Cortez is going to be pissed. Sam is either in a coma or had lost his mind. Carlos quickly alerted the guards to stop the drip and try to revive Sam. They untied him and took him to another room with a cot and laid him down. He was under nourished and dehydrated. His eyes just stared into space. They covered him with a blanket, but it was too late. Sam was completely unresponsive. They couldn't feel any pulse.

Frank was now suspicious and concerned. Cortez did not return his calls. It's now been a week and still no word from or about Carmen. It was time to act. He called in Alberto, his consigliere. Generally he does not involve his consigliere, whose main responsibility is to advise the boss on making impartial decisions based upon fairness and for the good of the family. Not personal matters or vendettas. However, this involved both a personal matter because it was his son, and Alberto's nephew. He needed advice from a personal aspect and the ramifications any move would have on the whole organization's interests. He also invited his under boss, Alex, who was his nephew. Frank laid out the whole situation. Alberto sat in silence. Alex was on the edge of his seat. Frank could see that Alex was already calculating a plan of action, which Frank feared would result in a blood bath. He looked at Alberto, waiting for a response. Alberto shifted in his chair.

This had all the implications of being a disaster. The last thing the family needed was a family war, Alberto thought. The organization was just fully recovering from the economic recession, and almost all the monetary setbacks it experienced. They needed to get more information before doing anything rash. Alex could be dangerous if they didn't' keep him controlled. He had a tendency to react before thinking and it usually involved violence. Finally, Alberto looked at Frank, who was staring intently at him. He suggested alerting the family soldiers, who are made-men and are the enforcers of the family and the Associates, who are not actual members of the family, but are involved with the criminal activities of the organization. They are drug dealers, assassins, lawyers, police informers, politicians, and anyone else on the organization's payroll. "Tell them to canvas all the areas where we do business. Question their snitches. Look under every rock and hiding place used by all their contacts to see if there is any trace or information on Carmen, or what happened to him. Use all the man power we have," Alberto said. "Hold off on any aggressive actions until we give our people and contacts time to gather any information." He looked at Alex as he said this. It was for his benefit. He knew Alex's temper. It is similar to Carmen's. After all, they were cousins. Frank thought for a moment. He too wanted to react immediately because this is his son they are talking about, but he agreed with Alberto to investigate before reacting. He gave the order to Alex. They would wait and see what would happen.

CHAPTER FIFTEEN

David was a little concerned because he hadn't heard from Emily since their dinner at the Labella. Her demeanor had changed, he thought, when she came out of the ladies room that night. He was convinced they had developed some sort of chemistry. All through dinner they laughed and talked like more than just friends. He felt a closeness and he thought she did too. He did not want the evening to end. She was once again very quiet on the ride home and said good night rather quickly, with no explanation. His phone rang interrupting his thoughts. It was Stone who said he needed to talk to him concerning new information on Sam. They met the next day for lunch. Stone told David that Carmen Leone, the son of organized crime boss Frank Leone, went missing, approximately the same time as Sam. Carmen and Sam are cousins, he told David. He also told David about the grave pits that were found in a remote field in Mexico. Quite a few bodies, but no way to identify any of them, according to the local police. What would Sam or Carmen be doing in Mexico? Stone also revealed that Frank Leone was under surveillance. Even though the family had legitimized most of their operation, they were still tied to several other illegal violations of the RICO Act. Stone said the information the FBI had from their sources could lead to Frank being tried for the crimes he ordered others to do. The FBI has been after Frank for years. Stone explained the Racketeer Influenced and Corrupt Organization Act, known as RICO, involves any violation of state statues against murder, gambling, kidnapping, extortion, arson, robbery, bribery, and dealing in a controlled substance. The law focuses specifically on racketeering and goes after the leaders of the organized crime family. The RICO Act closes the loop hole that allowed the boss to direct another member or associate of the family to commit a crime, thus exempting him because he did not actually commit the crime personally. With both missing family members, Stone expected foul play or a deal gone wrong. Once again David thought, what was Sam's connection to all this? Was Emily in danger? He asked Stone what his next action would be. Stone said his experience taught him to do nothing. These things eventually sort themselves out over time. They were waiting for Frank to make another mistake and see if anyone turned up dead. Months had passed since Sam and Carmen disappeared. Stone doubted any bodies would surface in the immediate future. He suggest that David do nothing either. Too much probing could prove to be dangerous.

CHAPTER SIXTEEN

Carmen was isolated in a small room with no windows. The walls were plain and no appliances were in the room. Not even a television. The bed was a twin with a stained mattress and a wool blanket. The men who brought him food never spoke to him. He had no idea how long he'd been there. He tried to remember if he had done anyone wrong lately or if it involved the family business. No one knew that he was headed to Mexico to firm up a deal with the Cortez's drug cartel except his Father and his bodyguard. Just then the door opened. One of the guards handed him a phone. He told Carmen to call his father and to tell him that he was fine, was busy seeing the operation, and loved the weather in Mexico. Carmen looked at him with questioning eyes. The guard took out a gun and placed the barrel against his temple. "Say exactly as I said, or you die, and so does your cousin," said the guard.

"My cousin," he wondered.

"What did any of my family members have to do with this? Were they captive too?" thought Carmen. His hands were shaking as he dialed. It rang several times before Frank answered. When he heard Carmen's voice a sigh of relief overwhelmed him.

"Where are you? You've had us all worried," said Frank.

"Everything is going as expected," replied Carmen. "The facility is large. The weather has been great. I'll be home soon. I have to go. They are waiting for me to have dinner. Tell mom I love her." He ended the call and handed the phone back to the guard.

Frank sat frozen. Carmen's mother has been dead for years. This could only mean one thing. Carmen was in trouble and he was letting Frank know. He quickly dialed Alberto and Alex. They both arrived at Frank's office a short time later. Frank told them of the phone call from Carmen. They agreed. Carmen had to be either held captive or on the run. He told Alex to see if he could determine the location of the call from his phone. Alex left the office to consul their contacts who are experts on tracing phone calls, in order to find out what they can find without revealing the situation. Alberto and Frank discussed their next move. Alex came back thirty minutes later and said the only info that his people could find out was the call was made from a burner, but it was made in the US, not from Mexico. Why would Carmen not use his own phone? Apparently someone did not want his location known. Carmen had a locator on his phone and either someone knew this or weren't taking any chances. Alberto suggested a search of Carmen's apartment to make sure he did not mistakenly forget to take his phone. They called Carmen's bodyguard, Marco, to see if he remembered if he saw Carmen's phone in his possession. They also wanted him to search the apartment.

Alex tried numerous times to reach Marco. He called Marco's favorite hangout, but the manager said he had not been in for days. The manager said the last time he talked to Marco, he told him he had to get up early to make a trip to the airport. He hasn't been in since. Either Marco has vanished or he set Carmen up. Marco was a made soldier. He has been with the family for a long time. He was as tough as they come and assumed as loyal also. Alex put the word on the street for any info on Marco. Was he with Carmen, or was he under a slab of concrete or the bottom of the river? He had to call Frank and let him know he could not find Marco.

The news that Carmen's bodyguard was missing sent Frank into a tirade. How could this happen in plain sight? Was there a conspiracy in his own family? Did someone sell him out to the cartel with which he was trying to establish a business arrangement? Cortez was avoiding him. He still wouldn't take Frank's calls. This is his son's life they are dealing with and he is most likely in danger. He had Alex check all the flights to Mexico. Carmen was aboard a flight to Mexico

City a week ago. Yet his call came from inside our own country. Possibly local. Frank called a meeting with all the family members. He was going to pull all the stops to find his son. He was going to send a party to Mexico to find Cortez's operation and, hopefully, find his son. He would flush out Cortez or any of his cartel members and get to the bottom of this mess. In Mexico, for the right amount of money, he could buy any person or information he needed.

Carlos was a nervous wreck. Cortez was going to go ape shit when he finds out their hostage is dead. They never got Sam to talk. He had to hand it to him, he was a tough hombre. He would rather suffer through pain and agony, then divulge any information. What loyalty. He doubted he could do the same. As it is, he is now concerned for his own well-being. He was delaying calling Cortez, but the guards knew and they could leak out that their prisoner was dead. He finally called and, as expected, Cortez was quite upset. Now, they may never know what Leone was up to sending an imposter into their camp. Cortez remembered his last conversation with Bartello. He implicated the Leone family trying to expand their drug market and possibly working with another cartel. *If this were true*, Cortez thought, *why would they negotiate with us? The whole thing didn't make sense, unless they were sending someone to see how our operation was run and where our weaknesses were.* A smart move sending someone resembling his son and not putting his own in harm's way. The imposter had all the correct identification to fool Carlos. Holding the imposter turned out to be a good move. It allotted them the time to discover that their captive was not Frank's son. Now all he could do was wait for Leone's next move. He told Carlos to strengthen the security at the manufacturing plant. Any move by another cartel could involve raiding their manufacturing and production building for a complete takeover of their operation.

Bartello called Diego Garcia as soon as he hung up from talking to Cortez. Cortez took the bait, Bartello told him. "The plan is working. Cortez is nervous and upset. He thinks the Leone family is undermining his operation and is in collusion with another cartel. He does not trust Frank Leone because he discovered that the person we sent as Leone's son was an imposter. He has no idea who you are.

I told Cortez that the word I got was a cartel out of Columbia is trying to move into the market. I also said that I was informed that the Leone family was trying to corner the whole drug market in the city. We still have Frank's son, Carmen, under wraps in case we need leverage or something goes wrong," said Bartello.

"What if their captive talks?" Garcia asked.

"Never will happen. I made him an offer when I sent him that I would protect his wife in his absence, but that if he disclosed any part of our plans, what I would do to her I described in vivid detail. He accepted. By the time we complete our move, I doubt he'll be alive. Now it's your turn to go into action," said Bartello.

Bartello had a tracking device put in Sam's watch. He figured that he would be searched and possibly body scanned, but they would probably remove his watch with the tracer undetected. His plan worked. He had a direct location of the drug manufacturing building. The trace was still on, so they never found it. He passed the information to Garcia. Garcia rounded up all the force he would need to take control of the site. He knew the place would be well guarded since Cortez felt betrayed by the Leone family. He needed a distraction. He used his paid contact on the local police to pull a surprise visit to the manufacturing site, under the pretense of a complaint from a local citizen from a small nearby village who saw smoke coming from the building. The contact would send two police cars to investigate, which would also be some of Garcia's men. Sort of a Trojan horse idea. Once his men were inside, the rest would storm the building. Now, all he had to do was wait for the men to arrive and get into position.

When Bartello's men grabbed Carmen, they knew they had to deal with his bodyguard. They waited outside Carmen's apartment building. Two men in a car and two men on the corner near the entrance. He emerged with his luggage and a large man who they assumed was Marco, his bodyguard by his side. The two men on the corner walked up behind them and put guns in their backs. Carmen and Marco stopped dead in their tracks. Was this a joke? Just then a black Escalade pulled up to the curb. One of the men ordered the two to get into the car. Marco immediately turned to confront the men. The one who was behind him shot him in the stomach. He fell against the man and they pushed him into the back seat. Carmen was petrified. They pushed him in beside Marco.

CHAPTER SEVENTEEN

David searched the internet to see if he could get any information about the grave pits Stone mentioned, found in a desolate area of Mexico. If the Leone family was dealing in drug trafficking and both Leone family members were missing, there could be a connection. His gut feeling said yes. But why Mexico? Did the Leone family have direct ties to a Mexican cartel? Stone was not telling him everything. Further research brought up an article about a major shoot out at a factory in a small remote area of Mexico months ago, which was close to the same time Sam and Carmen disappeared. No bodies were found, but there were gun shots and explosions heard by the villagers several miles away. The scene was described as a massacre site, blood everywhere, bullet shells, and casings all over the floor. Someone cleared out the bodies, but did not clean up the mess. The local police had no idea of what happened or were not divulging any information. According to the local police, the building had been vacant for years. *I wonder how much or what it took to silence the villagers nearby?*

Emily was becoming very frustrated with her state of affairs. She so wanted to move ahead with her life, but couldn't bring herself to give up on Sam. She could not get David out of her mind and she felt guilty because she officially was still married. She kept telling herself to give it more time. Now she wondered how she would react if Sam did come back into her life. David had sparked a feeling she had not felt in years. It made her contemplate what the rest of her life with Sam would be without feeling alive. He was so set in his ways and routines, that what he became was on the edge of bore-dom. A good man who forgot the romance and closeness that existed when they were first married. Do all marriages come to this after the honeymoon? Ten years is not a long time to be married, but lately it seemed like forever.

CHAPTER EIGHTEEN

Marco was bleeding profusely. He was slumped over and was withering in pain. He's not going to make it, Carmen thought. Apparently, they were not going to a hospital, but were heading to the east side of town. One of the kidnappers made a call to arrange to meet at the dock area. Carmen and Marco were wedged between two men in the back seat. Carmen tried to comfort Marco, but was told to shut up or he would wind up like his friend. When they arrived at the dock, several men were waiting for them. Marco was dragged from the car and that was the last time he saw his trusted friend who took a bullet for him. He assumed the men who dragged Marco out of the car were going to finish him off and discard his body in the river. He was struck in the back of the head and blacked out as the car drove off and headed to Bartello's safe house.

Frank was on the phone all day. He reached out to all his political contacts to have them put pressure on any agency they dealt with who would have connections with any new drug cartels. His soldiers and associates were beating the bushes and calling on every one of their snitches. So far, no news. Alex was preparing a team of men to fly to Mexico to find Cortez's operation. He knew Cortez must be covering something. He still was unreachable. Carmen's last known whereabouts was the airport headed for Mexico. Alex confirmed that Carmen was on the plane to Mexico City. How and when did he get back to make the phone call here in the US? The answers may be at Cortez's manufacturing operation. Alex, himself was leading the team. They would not be able to carry the arsenal they would need on the plane, so Frank made arrangements to have his connections in Mexico meet Alex and provide them with weapons. Seven men made up the team. Seven of the most loyal and dangerous men in Frank's organization. All were assassins. They were guys who worked their way up in the streets and buried many bodies along the way. They were all dressed in business suits and sat separately on the plane. They would work with local connections to find Cortez's operation. One thing Frank learned early in life; money and fear will buy anything or anyone.

Carmen tried to focus. He knew he should have been heading to Mexico when he was grabbed. Who would want to prevent him from going and why? No one knew he was going except his father, uncle Alberto, Alex, and his bodyguard, Marco. If Marco were involved in some treachery, he would not have been shot and lying at the bottom of the river. Alex was family and the under boss for Carmen's dad. It did not make sense. He did not recognize the men who captured him. Only another organized crime family would make a move this bold. There has been cooperation among the rival families and peace for years. Until the recession a few years ago, there was enough business transacted to keep everybody prosperous and happy. All the organizations felt the financial pinch back then, but most recovered, he thought. The only way that the existing families could survive today is to diversify and invest in legitimate businesses. A few held onto some of the old vices to generate a small cash flow. Frank had led the family through the tough times by keeping his drug distribution operation going. He said you always needed a sure thing to keep you afloat during emergencies and rough times. There will always be a market for drugs and alcohol. People always find a way to purchase them by hook or by crook. They will sell their children and their souls to satisfy their addiction. Carmen was sure that other families thought the same thing. Suddenly it hit him. He was about to solidify a deal with a major cartel to purchase a larger amount of drugs that would enable the family to secure a major share of the market. *What if another family heard of our plan and were trying to prevent the deal from happening?* thought Carmen. He hoped that his father would figure it out. Whether I'm around to know is any bodies guess.

Alex and his men got off the plane and took separate taxis to the rendezvous place where they would meet Frank's contact. The place was several miles from the airport at a large warehouse. Inside, a small, heavy man greeted Alex without introducing himself. He lead Alex and his men to a beat up, dusty old van and opened the back doors, revealing two cases containing guns and ammo, more than they hoped they would need. The heavy, small man told them to take what they wanted. Alex and his men took as much as they could carry. They loaded some extra weapons in the two cars that the small man had arranged for them to use. Just before they were about to leave, a large, heavy man came out of the shadows. He had on a police uniform and approached Alex. He was the chief of the local police. He was the brother-in law of the heavy, small man. He told them that the people and place they are looking for caused him to lose several of his fellow officers and close friends. The organization is run by one of the largest cartels in all of Mexico. Their leader is one of the most feared men in the whole country. He has failed to bring him to justice and stop his activities that are hurting his people and country. "If you can do what I could not, it would be a great blessing to us all," he said. "My brother in law has told me why you are here. I do not like your kind, who buy and sell drugs. Keep it in your country, so I will help you locate the drug manufacturing place you are looking for and hope you will all kill each other," he said. Alex explained that they were here to find a family member who they think was abducted by members of the cartel. The chief said it could only end in bloodshed.

Garcia recruited a small army of twenty five men. They were well armed. They were given instructions to eliminate everyone, other than the workers, but not to destroy any part of the facility. They needed the equipment and supplies to continue to run the operation. They needed to make it look like the Leone family arranged the takeover, so Cortez would retaliate against them. They loaded up and headed to the location Bartello gave Garcia. He gave the information to his right-hand man, who would lead the expedition. Garcia did not want to be seen or identified in case there were any survivors.

Alex and his men headed to a nearby motel to wait for word from the chief of police on the location of the cartel facility. He said he needed a few hours to make his contacts, who would know where the facility is. The men were tired and could use some rest after the long flight. They ate at a local cafe and played cards in their rooms. The men took turns guarding the cars and, being in an unfamiliar environment, for their own protection. At ten o'clock the chief came to the motel with another man, dressed like a peasant farmer. He said he was from the small village where an old building that looked like a warehouse was located an hour's drive away. The chief was convinced that this was the facility that the men were searching. The farmer said he has seen activity coming and going all hours of the day. He said he has smelled a strange odor every time he is near the place. He said he knows a few people in his village who apparently work there, but they are very secretive and never talk about their job. Some of the workers have disappeared over the years. He said he tends to a small piece of land where he grows enough food to feed his family and has several goats for milk. The chief told the farmer that these men would pay him handsomely if he took them to the warehouse near his village. They decided to leave early the next morning. Alex did not want to travel at night in strange surroundings.

Carlos doubled the guards at the plant. He felt that the location was safe and he did not have to worry. He did not think the secrecy of the location was breached. Cortez was probably over reacting. The cartel paid out a lot of money to ensure their privacy. He prohibited the workers from leaving. He kept them busy and worked them in shifts. He could not leave either. He had a small couch bed in his office. Cortez put the word on the street for all his soldiers and mules to be on the lookout for anything strange or out of the ordinary. He put his top people on alert. If and when the Leone family makes a move on the cartel, he wanted everyone aware and prepared. The last thing he needed was a war. No one benefits from the loss of lives and, most importantly, the loss of money through expenses to support the war, and the loss of income. If Bartello was right, Frank might make a move to secure their entire operation.

The next morning, the peasant farmer led Alex and his crew to within five miles of the warehouse. He could go no further for fear someone would see him. Alex gave the farmer a small wad of cash and he scurried away. They parked their cars in the high weeds, off the road in a large field, a mile from their destination. They proceeded slowly on foot. Two hundred yards from the building, they stopped and surveyed the area. Something did not look right. No one was in sight. They inched closer. No guards, no activity around the building, and no cars in the lot. Did they have the right location? Did the farmer and the police chief set them up or just take their money. It was almost ten o'clock in the morning and the sun was starting to get very hot. They sat there observing the building, looking for any sign of activity.

CHAPTER NINETEEN

At seven in the morning, Carlos was roused out of a sound sleep by one of his men. Two police cars had pulled up to the building. What could they want at this hour? Not another payday. It was too early in the month for that and too early in the day. Why two cars? The local chief usually came by himself and should be the only one who knows about the operation. It wasn't the chief, but another officer who identified himself as a deputy. He said the local villagers reported smoke coming from the building and thought there was a fire. They came to investigate. Carlos said there must be a mistake. Everything was fine and offered the deputy a beverage. Two of the deputy's men came in with him and Carlos noticed they were armed pretty heavily. Two others stood by the entrance door, also packing heavy heat.

Carlos's men were standing around listening to the conversation between the two men and were drinking coffee. The guards who were outside, came in to see what was going on and why the police were here. They were just milling around relaxing and enjoying their coffee after a long night on guard duty. Instinct hit Carlos like a ton of bricks. This was a hit and after all his precaution, they let their guard down. Suddenly the doors burst open and four other men in uniform charged in the room. They opened fire hitting three of Carlos's men, when a dozen more men piled into the building with blazing guns. Carlos took a bullet in his shoulder and another in his leg. He went down before he could get his gun out to shoot. His guards fled for cover, but there were too many assailants. His men could not match their fire power. They were surprised and outnumbered. The last thing Carlos saw as he laid in his own blood was the total massacre of his men. The battle lasted about five minutes. It was bloody and left the building in shambles. All the workers who survived the melee were ushered outside and made to haul all the bodies to a large truck with a huge bed. The truck was driven away to a remote area where the workers were forced to dig two large pits. The ground was hard so they needed two pits for all the bodies. After the pits were dug, and filled with the bodies of Carlos's men, the workers were lined up at the edge and executed and pushed in the open graves. Garcia's men then poured gasoline over the bodies and set them on fire. Between the fire and any wild animals, little trace would be left for the authorities to identify. This would surely cause Cortez to take action against the Leone Family. The only thing that went wrong, Garcia's man told him, was the building and equipment suffered some minor damages.

After deciding that the area outside the building was deserted, Alex's men moved cautiously forward, not knowing if anyone was inside. They spread out and flanked the building. As they got closer, they saw that the front entrance was open. Tracks indicated several vehicles must have left in a hurry. Tire marks indicated a large truck of some kind had pulled up to the front entrance. Two men went around to the back and looked through one of the only windows of an office equipped with a desk and furniture. It was empty. No sign of anyone. Alex and two of his men went in the front entrance and saw no trace of anyone either. What they did see is blood and ammo casings all over the floor. Bullet holes were in the interior walls. There must have been quite a battle just recently. Fresh blood was still puddled on the floor. This must have happened a few hours ago. They searched the building very carefully. They found dried coca leaves bundled in two rooms. Boxes were stacked in another room set up for packaging. All the processing equipment was still intact. There was only minimal damage from the gunfire. A great setup. *What went wrong between the cartel leader, Cortez, and my family?* thought Alex. He noticed a locked door to a small room in the back corner, opposite the office. He went into the office to look for a set of keys. The office must have been Carlos's, who he knew to be Cortez's chief of operations for the manufacturing of cocaine. It was made comfortable, probably because Carlos spent quite a bit of time here overlooking the production process. A set of keys were on the desk. Alex went back out to the locked door and opened it. He stepped back when the strong odor hit him. It was damp and pungent. A cot was in a corner with a body faced down. Whoever cleaned out all the dead bodies missed one. Alex lifted the blanket and turned the body over. He stood dead in his track. One of his men entered the room and saw the expression on Alex's face. It was one of horror and disbelief. The body was Carmen's. He did not expect to actually find Carmen here, but hoped to gain information of his whereabouts. Carmen's face was slightly sunken and dark circles around his eyes. He must have been tortured. He looked malnourished, dehydrated, and appeared to have been tortured. His clothes were wet. His eyes were open with a blank stare. "Gather any information you can from the office and send two of the men to get the cars. We need to take Carmen's body with us," Alex said. Two other guards came in the room and wrapped the body in a blanket and carried it to the front doors. Alex went into the office and assisted in searching for any information. He found Carmen's IDs in a desk drawer. "We need to clear out of here as soon as possible," Alex told his men. How were we going to get the body back to the States? As Alex was pondering how to get Carmen's body back to the states, one of his men told him they discovered several coffins in a storage room. Cortez must use them to ship drugs. He knows a favorite method of transporting drugs is using dead bodies. No authorities like to open a casket and have to deal with the unpleasant odors and the awkward position of dealing with family members. It would be the perfect way to get Carmen back home. He would need transportation for the casket from here to the airport. Good thing he found Carmen's identification papers, which contained his passport and return plane ticket. By a stroke of luck, one of his men found an old truck parked behind the building. The keys must be in the office somewhere. "I can hot wire the truck, if the battery's not dead. We can load the coffin in the back and cover it with a tarp I found," said one of his men.

"Good," said Alex. "Let's get out of here now."

The men were back with the cars. They loaded the casket and headed out, going directly to the airport. It would be at least an hour's drive. He called Frank and said "We found Carmen."

"In Mexico?" blurted Frank. "Yes, but I have bad news. Carmen is dead and we have his body," said Alex. Frank was stunned. How could this be? They thought he was in the states. "Are you sure the body is Carmen?" Frank asked out of desperation. "Yes, and we found all his identification papers. What we need you to do, Frank, is to make arrangements for us to bring the body home."

CHAPTER TWENTY

Frank called Alberto and told him he needed him immediately. The tone of Frank's voice could only mean trouble. Alberto was having lunch. He asked for the check and left quickly. He walked into Frank's office to find Frank in his chair bent over his desk with his head in his hands. Frank looked up with swollen eyes. What could bring Frank to tears? He was as tough as they come. Only one thing he could think of, they found Carmen and it was not good. "My son is dead, my son is dead," repeated Frank as if he were trying to deny it and had to convince himself otherwise. "What happened?" asked Alberto. "Alex called from Mexico, he said they found Carmen's body at Cortez's manufacturing building. He said they tortured him. My boy! Tortured and murdered. You must make arrangements for him to be shipped home. I can't bring myself to deal with it right now. I'm glad his mother's not alive to hear this. It would have killed her."

Frank and Alberto met the plane the next day. The hearse drove onto the tarmac. Alex and his men greeted Frank and extended their condolences. Frank stood stone faced as the casket was removed from the cargo hold of the aircraft and placed in the hearse. He hadn't got much sleep. His men helped load the coffin into the limo. He should have never sent Carmen to Mexico. He will regret this decision for the rest of his life. Frank wanted to ride back in the hearse to be with his son for the last time. Alberto and Alex rode together and the rest of the men followed in their cars. "What did you find at the facility?" asked Alberto. "It was deserted. No one around. We searched the building and only found Carmen's body. There was blood everywhere, so apparently a battle had to have taken place a few hours before we arrived. There were tire tracks all over the front lot. Someone cleared out the bodies, but did not clean up the blood. All the equipment seemed intact and the building had minimal damage, except for numerous bullet holes in the interior walls. Lots of casing and shells. We found Carmen's body in a locked room. He was laying on a cot in damp clothes. I don't know how long he'd been dead, but he was in terrible shape. We don't want Frank to be alone when he sees his body," said Alex.

They arrived at the funeral home and pulled around to the back door to unload the casket. The funeral director met Frank at the door and led him into his office. Alberto accompanied them and sat on a cushioned chair by the door. Frank sat opposite the director, who sat at his desk. "I am so sorry to be sitting here with you under these circumstances. I will do everything in my power to honor your son."

"Spare no expense," said Frank. "Prepare him to meet his mother in heaven. Make him beautiful for her eyes." The director said it would be his pleasure to honor such a request from a man he most admires and respects. He better do his best work, thought Alberto. Frank and the family are the only reason that he owned and operated a funeral home. He came to Frank ten years ago to borrow money to open his own business after he lost all his money in investments and gambling. His wife was about to leave him and take his kids. Frank saw a young man who needed a break, but had an addiction. He also figured he might need the director's services one day and he was a good source for disposing bodies. Frank gave him the money and told the man to never forget your family or put them in harm's way again, or he would have unmentionable things done to him. The man never swayed from dedication to the business and never gambled again. "Would you like to see your son now?" asked the director? "Yes, I am ready," said Frank. They walked to the embalming room where Carmen's body was on a table with a sheet draped over his body only exposing his face. Frank stood at the doorway with Alberto behind him. He had to gather all his strength to enter the room. Not since his wife passed away did Frank feel so helpless. He walked over to the table and gazed at Carmen's face. Startled, he backed away. "This is not my son," Frank exclaimed. "What?" said Alberto, moving closer to see the body. "This is not my son," Frank again shouted. The director looked at Alberto, then back at Frank. Even though the face was discolored and the skin drawn tight from dehydration and starvation, Frank knew that this was not Carmen. "I know my own son, this is not him. Who is this look alike?" Alberto saw a great resemblance to Carmen, but he too could see that this body was not Carmen. The director was speechless. Alberto left the room to find Alex. When Alex came into the room, he walked over to the table and looked at the body. "Was this the man you found in Mexico?" asked Frank. "It sure looks like him," replied Alex. "The body never left our sight. We watched the airline crew load the coffin on the plane. He sure looks like Carmen."

"Well, he's not. This means my son could still be alive. We need to find out who this person is," said Frank.

Diego Carcia received word from his top associate that the job was finished and all the evidence removed from the scene. No witness and very little damage to the facility. They left the imposters body locked in his room. When his body is discovered, he will be so decomposed that it will be hard for anyone to recognize him. Garcia called Bartello to give him the news. "Cortez would think that the Leone family was responsible for the attack and the body would be mistaken for Frank's son. This would surely pit the two against each other and break any deal between them. Now we would be able to control the manufacturing facility with the elimination of Carlos and his men. When do you want us to move in and set up shop?" said Garcia. Bartello thought for a moment. "Wait for me to get back to you. If we move too fast, there will be suspicion that we were involved. Let the two eliminate each other first. We still have Leone's son tucked away. We may need to throw him in the melee if they discover that the body is not Frank's son," said Bartello.

Alberto had the funeral director send the local forensic contact, who was also on Frank's payroll and is Frank's personal physician, a sample of DNA from the body. "Maybe he was in the system and we could get a hit on his identity," said the doctor. The funeral director personally delivered the sample. The Doctor called Alberto and said he would have an answer in a few days. Alberto gave instructions to only call him with the results and to not let this leak out. The doctor knew better than to open his mouth when it came to any business involving Frank or his family.

Cortez could not reach Carlos. He seemed to vanish from the earth. He did not want to risk going to Mexico to find him. His local contacts told him there was no activity at the warehouse/manufacturing plant. Cortez called Bartello to see if he heard any more about the new cartel that is rumored to be courting the Leone Family. Cortez was really stressed now. If something happened at the plant, he was in danger of losing Bartello's business. He is Cortez's largest buyer. He had not told Bartello about Sam. Bartello did not tell Cortez about Carmen's abduction. Bartello was watching Cortez come apart and waiting for Frank to strike out against Cortez's cartel. What a great view Angelo had of the whole situation. He was sitting back, waiting for the smoke to clear and he would control the whole drug market in the city. "I've heard nothing," was Bartello's answer.

It's been almost two weeks since Carmen and Marco went missing and Frank was starting to put the pieces together. Why did someone impersonating my son go to Mexico in Carmen's place? Frank started to put the pieces together. Carmen goes missing and someone impersonating him goes in his place. Someone did not want Carmen in Mexico, who would be representing me. But why send an imposter. He looked enough like Carmen to fool most people. Did some other group want their man inside Cortez's operation to gain information? How did they come by such a look alike? Were they trying to kill Frank's dealings with Cortez's cartel? Who would have the most to gain by stopping Frank from expanding? His biggest competition for the drug trafficking is Angelo Bartello's family. His, like Frank's family, is one of the oldest organizations around. So who took Carmen?

Alberto called Frank. "Your doc told me he has some interesting information for us. Too delicate to discuss over the phone. Can you meet me at his office in an hour?"

"Okay," Frank answered. He called his driver to pick him up in thirty minutes. Alberto was already at the office sitting in the waiting room. As soon as Frank walked in, they were whisked away to the doctor's private office by one of the receptionists. The doctor walked in a few minutes later. He looked directly at Frank and said he had the report back on the DNA sample they gave him. He hesitated for several seconds, then simply said, "The man has your family DNA."

"What did you say?" Frank and Alberto came forward in their seats at the same time. "I said the DNA indicates he is your relative," said the doctor. Frank and Alberto sat speechless. "I used a sample of DNA from your records, Frank, to make the comparison. I did not find anything in the data base, but when Alberto told me how much he looked like Carmen, I compared the DNA. He is related to you both and judging by his age, he is probably your nephew." The doctor didn't know who was more surprised, Alberto or Frank.

Alberto and Frank left the office in silence. They went back to Frank's office without exchanging a word. Alberto was the first to speak. He had been going over the family tree in his mind on the drive back. "Whose child could he be? Who in the family have we not been in touch with over the last so many years? Who most resembled Carmen when they were younger? Could the person be an illegitimate child of one of our brothers? Or one of our sisters?" asked Alberto. Frank was still taken in by what he just learned. "Our parents had seven boys and eight girls with children scattered everywhere," said Frank. "I probably could not recognize half of our nieces and nephews I haven't seen for years. I don't recall any of them ever looking like Carmen enough to be his twin. The only one of our brothers and sisters we lost touch with years ago was our sister Sonia. You remember she married that non Italian, Michael Carson, which upset mom and pop. They had a son, Samuel, whom she named after our oldest brother. The last time I saw him was when he and Carmen graduated college. After Sonia and Mike passed away, I lost touch with Sam. I don't remember Carmen talking about him lately either. I remember he rejected our offer to join the family business. A smart kid who would have been a great contributor if his father had not influenced him to steer clear of our family's organization. Mike not being Italian, did not agree with our lifestyle and the way we make our living," said Frank. "Sam was a good kid," said Alberto. "Mike was a hard worker. Remember when he worked for our brother Sam's construction company? He always worked several jobs to keep a roof over Sonia and the boy's head. He would never accept help from us. Too proud. He should have been Italian. Didn't we hear some time ago that Sam got married? I think Carmen mentioned it a while back. Maybe his wife or family can shed some light on this. We should have kept track of him. Sonia would have wanted us to," said Alberto.

The funeral director kept Sam's body on ice as directed by Alberto. He had no clue who this man was, and, by Frank and Alberto's reactions, he did not want to know. Now, he was worried about having a dead body that no one knew was in his possession. He could not hold the body for too long. It must be disposed of or prepared for a funeral. All Frank had done for him could be gone in an instant if anyone discovered he was hiding a body. An investigation would cost him his business. This person was murdered, anyone could tell.

Alberto reached out to his contact with the local police. He wanted a thorough search of all police, hospital, medical records and missing person reports for a Samuel Carson, who was Caucasian, between the ages of thirty five to forty. Alberto did not even know Sam's birth date. "Give me a couple days and I'll call you back," the officer replied. Frank let Alberto do the searching for their nephew. He needed to figure out Cortez's or Bartello's next move. Alex said the plant in Mexico was deserted and no signs of activity. Where was Carmen?

Garcia was anxious to start production at Cortez's manufacturing plant. He already paid off the local politicians and had a source in the police department on his payroll. They did not care who had control of the warehouse, as long as they received their payoff. The villagers would not come near the place, and, they kept their mouths shut out of fear. Garcia was going to import his own labor force. He would set up living quarters in the facility. There was plenty of room and he could prevent them from outside contact. His workers were poor and needed money for their families. He would arrange for them to send the little money they earned to their families and provide all the essentials for the workers at the warehouse. If the workers knew their families were provided for, they would be loyal employees. Now, Garcia needed to start generating some income. He had the pledge from the Bartello family, who promised Garcia the whole city market, plus other cities that Bartello had connections in on the east coast. His other operations were small compared to this one. He would quickly become the leading cartel drug distributer. He already had his men pushing hard to cover the loss of product for Bartello's family. Cortez's supply was apparently dwindling and he was having trouble covering his regular customers' needs.

Cortez knew he had taken a big hit. His local supply was running out of drugs. Bartello got all over his case because his men were not able to get their normal shipments of drugs to sell. The streets were getting restless. The flow of drugs was getting slow. All the way down to the lowest junkies were feeling the crunch. The dealers were losing income. Everyone was feeling the pinch. It just took days to have an effect. The only one who was holding their own was the Leone family. Their dealers were still being supplied. He knew Frank had a supplier, but he told Cortez he needed to expand his share of the market. It was probably the group from Columbia. They were trying to move into the east coast market. Frank was behind this whole mess, thought Cortez. Either his men or the Columbian cartel took out the Mexican operation. Either way, Frank was involved. He figured his top associate, Carlos, was dead or sold him out, and was with the new cartel. He called a meeting at his local distribution warehouse with his top dealers." We need to take out Frank Leone," he said.

Bartello knew it wouldn't take Cortez long to act. Cortez was going after Frank. If he takes Frank out, he'll alienate all the families in the city who do not want a war. It's never good for anyone's business. If Frank takes him out, some of the families will lose a supplier and will suffer an income loss, which might be enough to initiate a war. Either way, Bartello is in the driver's seat. He gets rid of competition and gains control of the drug market. He called his top man, Joey Pataglia. "Come over and celebrate with me, Joey, we are about to become the industry leaders of the city," said Bartello.

CHAPTER TWENTY-ONE

David was reading about the grave sites found in Mexico, still try-ing to make a connection with Carmen's and Sam's disappearances when the phone rang. It was Emily. "Am I interrupting anything?" she asked.

"No, I was about to go get a bite to eat. Would you like to join me?" asked David.

"Sure," she replied. "I was getting hungry and needed a break too. I was going through Sam's clothing to see if there could be any info we may have not seen. I didn't find anything except some money and tissue in his pockets. I guess I'm bored. Where do you want to eat?" she asked. "How about pizza and beer again where we went last time?" said David.

"Fine," said Emily. "I'll see you in twenty minutes."

Emily was waiting when David walked in the pizza shop. They sat in a rear booth. There were few customers now. It was well after lunch time. Emily stared at him for a few moments with a quizzical look. "I was thinking about what you told me about Sam's back-ground and his family's ties to organized crime," she said." Oh no, David thought, I don't like where this is heading. "What if we contact his family and see if they have any information they are not coming forward with about Sam?" she suggested. He was right. It was headed in a bad direction. He did not tell her about Carmen being missing around the same time as Sam. At least he didn't remember telling her. "Maybe they don't even know. Wouldn't they have ways to find out things that the police couldn't?" she asked. *How do I control this situ-*

ation? he pondered. *This could be very dangerous. How can I avert this from happening.* "Look, Emily, that could be very dangerous poking around in the crime family organization asking questions. Let me call Stone again and see if he has any contacts who could find out if Sam's family knows anything. My guess is that if Sam hasn't had any contact with his family that you know about, chances are they don't even know he disappeared. Let's eat and relax and forget about the case for now," David said. Their pizza arrived and they ate and drank their beer. It was great to see her again. She was thinking the same thing about him.

David went back to his office and did some more digging into the time period. It was almost six months ago that the mass grave sites were found in Mexico. He vaguely remembered reading something about a cartel drug lord who was assassinated shortly after the grave pits were found. He found the story online. A Javier Cortez was gunned down over a drug deal gone bad, was how it was reported. The FBI reported that he operated one of the largest cartels out of Mexico. Reports suggested that one of the organized crime families was responsible. The report over the next few days said that the local police reported finding bodies, believed to be Cortez's men, in a warehouse near the dock. They found money and drugs scattered around, as if a major deal ended in a fire fight or someone was extracting revenge. "Why didn't Stone tell me about this?" said David.

CHAPTER TWENTY-TWO

The next day, Alberto's inside police contact called. "It did not take much digging. His named popped up on the missing person's report filed by his wife last week. She claimed he never came home and she hasn't heard from him. A detective, Tim Becket, handled the case. I reached out to him this morning and he was not very forthcoming with any information. He said he thought he was dead or took off with another woman, which usually happens on these types of disappearances. No ransom calls or notes. He was an upstanding guy as far as Becket could tell from a background search he did. Maybe he got tangled up with the wrong crowd. He was a real estate broker, so maybe he pissed someone off. That's all I can tell you," the contact said.

Missing, thought Alberto. *No coincidence.* This was Samuel, my sister's boy. How did he get tied up in all this? Alberto called Frank and told him what he found out about Sam. "The body is Samuel, our nephew," said Alberto. Frank's mind was racing. "We need to give him a proper burial," Frank said. "A very private one. There will be too many questions to answer if it becomes public. He's our blood and the authorities will think he is connected to our organization. Even his wife must continue to think he is missing. Him turning up dead in our possession would bring too much attention on us. Make arrangements to have him buried in the family cemetery in an unmarked grave," said Frank.

Sam's body was placed in an unmarked grave in the far corner of the small cemetery that the family owned. They had purchased the plot sites years ago, enough for all the family members and their children. The only ones in attendance were Frank, Alberto, and Alex. They couldn't trust a leak from any of the other family members. Some day they may all learn of Sam's fate, but for now it needed to be kept secret. Sam was kidnapped by the Cortez cartel and he didn't want them to know he found Sam. Frank knew Cortez kidnapped Sam. It all made sense. He was also sure they had Carmen somewhere and were keeping him alive for leverage. He would bring down the whole cartel. His men were scouring the whole city to find Cortez's local distribution point. This brought back memories of long ago when the families went to war. He knew his drug income would suffer, but he had to establish respect in his world of organized crime and get revenge. He knew someone always steps up to take over when someone goes down. There is probably a new cartel waiting to emerge.

Bartello and Pataglia were sitting in Angelo's office gloating about the success of their plan to destroy Cortez and the Leone family. "How is Carmen faring?" asked Bartello. "We keep him groggy with drugs, but just enough to keep him quite. How long do we need him?" asked Pataglia.

"My guess is that Frank found Sam's body. Since the police made no mention of the body, Frank's men got it. That was a good move on Garcia's men's part, leaving the body. He is probably making plans to hit Cortez. Is Garcia ready to take possession of the manufacturing plant in Mexico?" said Bartello. "He's waiting for your word," said Pataglia."

"Then give him the okay. With Leone in action it will be a distraction for Garcia to set up. We need the flow as soon as possible to hit the city. The natives are getting restless," said Bartello.

Frank's men surprised Cortez and his men. One of Cortez's men gave up the location of their local operation. He was a small-time dealer who succumbed to heavy interrogation. He led Frank's men to the receiving and distribution center. Alex led the assault. His men were heavily armed and caught Cortez and his men by complete surprise. It lasted just a few minutes. Cortez was in his office with his top associate when the Leone family henchmen stormed in with guns blazing. Cortez ran for a backdoor exit, where he was hit by two men waiting outside the door. They shot him several times to Alex's disappointment. He wanted Cortez alive. Alex was hoping they would find Carmen there or get Cortez to tell them where Carmen was. The location was in an isolated area up the river on the north side of town. They searched the entire building, but no sign of Carmen. "Leave everything here. Bodies, drugs, money, leave it all. This will send a message to Cortez's partners and associates that we will stop at nothing to recover what is ours," Alex told his men. They left as quickly as they came.

David called Stone and questioned him on what the FBI knew of what he found on the internet about the drug lord assassination and the suggested ties to an organized crime family. "Was Sam or Carmen found among the bodies and you're not telling me? I get the feeling that you are keeping something from me," said David. Stone was quiet for a moment. "David, we think it was the Leone family who made the hit on Cortez and his operation. Frank's son Carmen went missing at the same time that Sam did. You know they are related. Our information tells us that both are probably dead since neither one has surfaced after all this time. We are not sure of what happened in Mexico, or who made that hit. It may have been a rival cartel. Someone took over the drug distribution that Cortez had. The market is being supplied. We think it is a group out of Columbia. As far as the massacre on the north dock warehouse, our sources tell us it was the Leone family," said Stone. "I have a real predicament Robert," David said. "Emily wants to approach the Leone family to get information on what they know about Sam being missing. I told her about Sam's background and family ties. Not good I know, but I think she deserves closure."

Stone retorted, "You know that is a dangerous move. I know it's her husband we are talking about, but if they did not reach out to her by now, they don't trust her. After all, they haven't had a relationship with her before this. As far as we know they have never met."

Diego Garcia did not take long to get his operation going in the new Mexican location of Cortez's operation. Once he received the information that Cortez was dead, he moved in and set up his distribution outlet. With his Columbian trade now firmly implanted in Mexico, he could control all the trafficking to the major US markets. Angelo Bartello was his main buyer. The Leone family was trying to make roadways into the drug market, but they lacked a major supplier. They were taking a low profile after the Cortez assassination. They were still looking for answers of Frank's son's disappearance. As promised, Bartello introduced Garcia to some other big-time buyers in other cities. Bartello's plan was working. He was squeezing the Leone family out of the market.

Word on the street got back to Frank that a new supplier was in town. He tried to reach out to them to strike a deal to replace the one that didn't work out with Cortez's cartel. The flow of drugs that Cortez had been supplying was still moving, which indicated a new cartel had been established. The Leone family needed a major supplier. Whatever the cartel's name is, or who the leader is has been a mystery. Frank's family soldiers and associates, who are criminals who work for the family, but are not part of the organization, told Alex that their dealers were being pushed out of the market. Their territories were dwindling. They couldn't meet the demand for supplies and were losing business to another supplier. Frank had his suspicions, that another family was behind his problem. Frank was never greedy. He believed in taking his share, but also to leave a little for the next guy. Their certainly was enough demand for drugs to go around in most of the large cities. Someone was trying to control the market. The new cartel could not have moved in and established itself without the help of another powerful organization. The new cartel ignored all of Leone's advances and attempts to recognize the Leone Family. Cortez's warehouse on the north river dock was under observation by the police and has been vacant since Alex's attack. Finally, Frank got a break. His contact with the local police called Alberto. "Something I thought you should know. Our narcotics squad busted a buy on the north side, in a body shop, owned by one of Joey Pataglia's associates. We had been watching the place and suspected that it was also a chop shop. One of the detectives during a stake out noticed one of the local drug dealers, who we had arrested, frequenting the place. He alerted the narcotics department and they investigated the shop. One of their undercover agents made contact with the dealer and found out that a buy was going to take place. This was where the local small-time dealers got their suppliers each week. When our men made the bust, they confiscated fifty grand and two kilos of cocaine. I don't know if this information helps or not, but I wanted to pass it along to you," said the contact. Alberto replied, "Thank you. Look for a little extra in your envelope next week." *We had our answer*, thought Alberto. *The Bartello family has to be behind the new cartel. Joey Pataglia is Bartello's right-hand man.* He called Frank with the information they had suspected all along.

Frank was sure now that the Bartello family had something to do with Carmen's and Samuel's disappearance, now that Cortez was dead. "If Pataglia's associates were getting drug supplies, then the new cartel had to be dealing exclusively with Bartello's family," Frank told Alberto. "Just like Angelo to buy up the market! He pitted me and Cortez against each other and created a lack of trust between us. Cortez probably thought we sent an imposter to negotiate, instead of my son. When he found out Sam was not Carmen, he took this as an act of mistrust and thought we were trying to get information and find his location for other purposes. Since Sam had all of Carmen's identifications, someone had to have taken them from Carmen. This could only have been Bartello. He has to have Carmen or know where he is. I think he is still alive. Bartello is keeping him alive for insurance, in case we put together his scheme. He knocks off competition in the market and establishes a new supplier for himself only. He must have found out that we were negotiating a deal with Cortez. He also must have made advanced moves to set up a new carte, and they are probably the ones who took out the manufacturing plant in Mexico. That's why we can't make any headway with the new cartel. Now the problem is, what do we do about this?"

Alberto answered, "Nothing right now. We need to lay low. After all the bloodshed, and bodies turning up, we need to take a low profile. Our other investment incomes are steady so we can hang in there for a while. Let the dust settle."

"What about Carmen?" asked Frank.

Carmen was blindfolded and driven to a new location. Bartello wanted to keep Carmen in good health now that everything had gone according to plans. He was insurance and a bargaining chip. Bartello knew from experience that anything could go wrong at any time. Anyone could be bought and he trusted very few people. Betrayal was a common act when pressured to make a deal when criminals were captured or caught by authorities or other families. Just a handful of his most trusted soldiers knew about Carmen. The new safe house was a total upgrade from the one room cell. Carmen took a long leisurely shower, something he hadn't had in days. He was given fresh clothing and a good meal. The bed was large and comfortable. The windows were sealed and blackened so he could not see out, nor could anyone see in the window. Carmen felt better about his chances of survival now that he was made to feel more comfortable. He was sure his father, Frank, understood his message. His mother has been dead for years. He asked one of the guards, whom he recognized as one of the men who kidnapped him, what happened to Marco, his bodyguard? "He's at the bottom of the river where you will be if you don't shut your mouth," was his reply.

It has to be at least a week—he lost track of time—*since they grabbed me*, Carmen thought. *Obviously, they need me alive*, he thought. He wondered how long they would keep him hostage. He had no idea of all the moves that transpired in the last week or so.

CHAPTER TWENTY-THREE

Emily was going through Sam's things reminiscing about their life together, but mostly she was plotting and planning on how exactly she could get in touch with or approach Sam's extended family: the notorious Leone crime family. All she knew about them was what David had told her. Even though she never met them, surely they would accept her, since she was married into the family. Sam was usually very open about his past, but he'd claim up when it came to talking about his mother's family. The fact that he never talked about his family is understandable, now that she knows their history of organized crime involvement. His character would never approve of their life style. She truly believed that his disappearance was due to his family ties. Her phone rang, interrupting her thoughts. It was David. He was worried that she was so frustrated that she just may try to approach the Leone family. She wanted closure. He called her to gauge her temperament. "Hi Emily, would you like to go have a beer with me? Maybe go to a show, just to get you out for a while? Kind of take your mind off thinks," he asked.

"I'd love to just have a beer and talk, if that's okay?" said Emily. David said that would be great. "I'll pick you up in twenty minutes."

Emily threw on a pair of jeans and a sweatshirt. She didn't have enough time to fix her hair, so she threw on a visor. When she came out of her house, David was amazed at how great she could look in anything. He loved her casual, simplistic look. She could look good in farmer's overalls. He opened her door and she smiled and thanked him. They drove to a bar a few miles away. Inside they sat at a booth in the back. She reached out her hand for his. His heart jumped. "David, I really need your help to reach out to Sam's family. I can't proceed with my life until I get closure. I feel that he's gone, but I've got to know for certain. I think the Leone family knows what happened to him. I understand that I may find out things that may not be pleasant. I know I could be opening a can of worms, but I can't see them doing any harm to me. I am or was married into the family. Before you answer, I want you to know, I have feelings for you. Serious feelings. But until I can put this behind me, I will always feel guilty about any romantic relationship I enter into. So please help me. If you care about me also, we both need to know." She squeezed his hand and looked into his eyes. David knew she was right. He could never have a true relationship with her. He would always be fighting Sam's ghost. She would never fully succumb to a relationship without closure. He knew she wanted him as much as he wanted her, so for this to happen they had to find an end to the disappearance. "Well, the way I see this is, it is one either they reject you, two they don't know where he is, or three they help you," David said. "I guess this is probably your last option. I don't like it, but you know I want to take our relationship further. If this gets us there, then I will help you." David couldn't help but wonder, what if Sam is still alive and came back into her life? How would he handle that?

CHAPTER TWENTY-FOUR

After burying his nephew, Frank jumped right into researching Angelo Bartello's recent family activities. He knew Bartello was a long time boss of one of the most powerful organized crime families in the city. He knew that Bartello had connections all over the country and had many politicians in his pocket. Their families had always respected each other and honored each other's territories. Why this sudden move on Bartello's part? Alberto sat across from Frank in his office. "Tell me, Alberto. You're supposed to be my consigliere, my advisor, my confidant, so advise me. What should we do? We have been patient and quiet for months now. No sign of Carmen. Our drug trade is barely hanging on and there's no word on the street about the mysterious cartel supplying the whole market. Our dealers are forced to buy from Bartello's associates. He has the city pretty much tied up. It's time we put the squeeze on some of his people for some answers. We have to assume Carmen is dead. Marco never surfaced, so he is probably dead too. I can't sit here any longer doing nothing. We have been silent for too long, so maybe we can catch Bartello off guard." Alberto nodded. "Let's bring Alex in. Send him out to get some answers. Put pressure on till someone breaks," said Alberto.

Carmen was going stir crazy. He did not have a TV, so he had no idea of what was going on in the world. He slept, showered, and ate. No communication with anyone. The guards entered and left his room quickly. How long he has been held captive, he has no idea. It feels like months. He knew his family has to be looking for him. He knew he must be drugged. He felt he was losing his senses. Bartello knew of Carmen's reputation and his notorious temper and how violent he could be about things. Bartello doubted any of Carmen's men missed him. Carmen would strike out at the slightest thing that irritated him. Most of the time it was at one of his men. Bartello was hoping Carmen's men would not be too anxious to have Carmen back and would not be looking too hard to find him.

Alex took three of his most trusted, dangerous henchmen and started making visits to some of the small-time dealers who worked for Pataglia's associates. At first, he was diplomatic in order to not spread fear and send the dealers into hiding, or seeking Pataglia's protection. He acted like he was just trying to make a score. He was not known to the small dealers, but he had to be careful that he was not recognized by any of Pataglia's or Bartello's men. After weeks of searching, he stumbled on Jingo, an old drug dealer he knew from years ago. The guy was a junkie. The only reason he was still selling, was to be able to acquire drugs for his own habit. He didn't recognize Alex. Alex figured he couldn't recognize anyone in his shape. Jingo looked one coke away from death or whatever drugs he's into, which was probably all the time, when Alex caught up to him. He looked like he had been through World War Three. His face was withered and his cloths were worn and old. He worked the south side of the city, dealing in the projects and the surrounding nearby dilapidated neighborhood. They lured him over to their car and threw him in the back seat. "Hi Jingo, we want to buy some information. I know you buy from Joey Pataglia's dealers. I need you to tell me where you pick up you drugs," said Alex. "I don't know nothing," replied Jingo. "Let me tell you what I know. You will not leave this car alive if you don't cooperate," said Alex. "What's in it for me?" asked Jingo. "A nice cash reward, if you tell me what I want to know," said Alex. "Where do you get your supply?"

"I go to the body shop," said Jingo.

"What body shop?" asked Alex.

"You know, the one on the strip," said Jingo.

"Whose shop is it?" asked Alex.

"I don't know," said Jingo.

"I'll ask one more time. Whose shop is it?" asked Alex.

"Some dude they call JR. I don't know his name," replied Jingo.

"Is he the one who gives you your supply?"

"Yeah," said Jingo.

"Who does he work for?" asked Alex.

"I heard them talk about some guy called Pag something. When I was waiting for my bag, I heard them say the big boss wasn't happy."

"Did you hear the name Pataglia?"

"Yeah, I think that's it."

"What was he unhappy about?"

"Something about the cops watching the place."

"What else?"

"JR said he had to deliver a package to Pag's, whatever his name was, men, for some guy they had to keep quiet, maybe a police man or somebody they take care of."

"Was the package drugs?" asked Alex.

"I don't know man," answered Jingo. "I just hear things because they think I'm out of it half the time which I am. They don't care what they say in front of me. They think I'm always strung out. All I care about is getting my bag."

"Good work Jingo. Here, don't spend it all in one place. Don't tell anyone about our conversation or we'll be back. You understand?"

Alex told Frank and Alberto about this conversation with Jingo. The plan was to put a tail on JR. It could be that the person Jingo mentioned to keep quiet was Carmen. It was a lead worth following. If he were stashed somewhere, they had to have him drugged to contain him. Alex put two men on watch detail. Bartello or Pataglia would not trust just anyone to deliver anything to where they had Carmen. Alex guessed that only a few select men would know the location. He instructed his men to look for anyone unusual coming and going from the shop. The police were watching the shop, so they had to be careful not to draw their attention. Alex's two men sat on the shop for a week, when, one day, they failed to report in. Alex sent his men to check on the pair. They found their car five blocks from the shop. No one was inside. They popped the trunk and found both men dead with their throats slashed.

Frank decided it was time to take action against the Bartello family. He instructed Alex to have Joey Pataglia's man, JR, who runs the auto body shop, grabbed and taken to the funeral home, operated by Frank's associate. "Let me know when you get him. Take him to the basement and secure him there. I want to personally question him," said Frank.

Johnny Rizzo, known as JR left the shop at ten thirty and headed home with a small bag of weed. He was going to have a relaxing night and get high. He was the last to leave the shop and locked up the drugs and the money in the safe. He drove down Second Avenue, as usual, when a black sedan pulled up beside him. The driver motioned for JR to wind down his window. Out of nowhere a truck pulled in front on JR's car and slammed on his brakes. JR rammed into the back of the truck. The next thing he knew he was being dragged from his car and thrown into the back seat of the sedan. Two men grabbed his wrists and tied him up. One of them put a gun to JR's head and told him to be quiet. They drove off and headed to the funeral home where Frank would meet them. They drove around back, where the director let them inside. They pulled JR from the car and lead him to the basement. There was a long stainless steel table in the middle of the room. The two guards forced JR on the table and strapped him down. One of the men took off JR's shoes and socks. On a sink in the corner was a set of tools. "What am I doing here? Do you know who I work for?" yelled JR.

The two guards ignored him. "I work for a well-connected family who are going to be very pissed off if you don't let me go."

"Shut up," said one of the guards, "or I'll cut off your foot."

Frank and Alex arrived and went directly to the basement. JR was now terrified. Two thugs and two men in expensive suits could not be good. "What's your name?" asked Frank. "Look, I don't know what you want but you have the wrong guy. I just run a body shop," said JR. "I'll ask again, what's your name?"

"Johnny Rizzo."

"Johnny, do you know Joey Pataglia?" asked Frank. "I've heard his name," answered JR. "Don't lie to me Johnny. It's very disrespectful. Now, tell me how you know Joey Pataglia?" said Frank.

"I think he owns the body shop," said JR.

"Do any of Pataglia's men come in the shop?" asked Frank.

"I don't know. I don't know who they are," said JR.

"Johnny, you're not telling me the truth and it's very upsetting to me. Tell me the truth, or one of my men will cut off one of your toes," threatened Frank.

JR lay motionless. Frank nodded to his man by the sink, who picked up a pair of cutting pliers. He took JR's foot and snipped off the little toe of his left foot. JR screamed in pain and shock.

Frank yelled over JR's screams, "Tell me or lose another toe."

JR withered on the table. "Yes, his men come in!" screamed JR.

"What do they come in for?" asked Frank.

"They pick up a small bag of drugs," sobbed JR.

"For who?" asked Frank.

"I don't know, honest," said JR.

"You're lying again," and Frank motioned to his man to cut off another toe.

"Stop please, they need it for someone they have. Someone they watch, that's all I know," said JR in pain."

"Where is this man they are keeping watch over?" asked Frank.

"I don't know. Sometimes I deliver it to them at the parking garage on the corner of Riverside and Union. I think they walk to meet me, so it must not be far. Sometimes they come to the shop. That's all I know," said JR.

"What day do they make the pickup?" asked Frank.

"On Fridays mostly," JR answered.

"Thank you, Johnny Rizzo, was that so hard?" Frank commented. Frank turned to his men and calmly told them to dispose of JR.

CHAPTER TWENTY-FIVE

Frank had hope that Carmen might still be alive. We now have a possible location to check out, he thought. They must be holding Carmen in one of the buildings near the garage. We have to move fast. When JR came up missing, they might get spooked and move Carmen. He had to figure out a way to post surveillance in the area without tipping his hand. He had Alberto contact one of the city officials who was on their payroll. He needed building plans for a two block area. If Pataglia's men walked to meet JR at the garage for the exchange, it couldn't have been far. Like most bodyguards or family associates, they would prefer to drive to locations, rather than walk. They generally weren't in the best shape. Frank's best guess was that Carmen would be in a two block area. With the building layouts in front of them, Frank and Alberto spent the next two hours poring over the plans. Eight buildings were businesses with no living quarters. Six buildings were small apartment complexes. The one building that caught Frank's attention was a small condo with access from an alley, next to a vacant lot. It could be a good place for anyone to get in and out without being noticed. Alberto set out to find who owned the building.

Alberto found out the condo was titled under the name Blue Sky Enterprise. "The signature on the title has Joey Pataglia as managing partner for the corporation. What a coincidence," Alberto said sarcastically. "Get a crew together. We're going to hit that building tonight, before they catch on that were on to them. If they have Carmen, then this will be our best chance to get him back," said

Alberto. At eleven o'clock that evening, seven of Alex's men in two cars pulled up a block away from the condo, behind a large apartment building. Two men got out and headed in opposite directions to spot for any lookouts. Two of Pataglia's men were sitting in a car in front of the condo. They were the only men on guard. Joey must feel pretty confident that his hide out was secure. It took ten seconds for Alex's men to terminate the guards without a sound. The rest of Alex's men moved slowly, in the shadows, surrounding the condo. The second floor lights were on. Alberto's city hall connection provided Alberto with the condo floor plan. It was a two bedroom complex, with both bedrooms on the upper floor. Odds were that Carmen would be keep locked in one of the bedrooms. The windows in the back bedroom had been blacked out. That's got to be where Carmen is. "I hope Carmen's alone when we storm in the building. His best chance of survival is if he is in the bedroom and all the men are downstairs," Alex said. With all his men in position, they assailed the building. The first two men broke in the front door. Two others smashed the rear windows and fired into the rooms. Pataglia's men were caught completely off guard. Two more of Alex's men rushed upstairs to the bedrooms, with Alex trailing behind. One of the bedroom doors was open. No one was inside. Alex kicked down the closed door of the other bedroom and found Carmen laying on the bed half conscious. He looked like he'd been heavily sedated with drugs. His clothes looked, as if he had been sleeping in them for days. His face was ashen and drawn. He probably had more drugs in his system than food. "Grab him and let's go!" shouted Alex over the gun fire from below. They carried Carmen down the stairs and out of the front door to a waiting car. They shoved him in and sped off. The carnage inside the condo was loud and bright. All of Pataglia's men were killed. The whole operation lasted less than three minutes. Alex's men retreated quickly and vanished into the night.

Frank was waiting at the funeral home. Alex called as soon as he retrieved Carmen and was heading to meet Frank. Frank paced the floor. He was assured by Alex that Carmen was alive, but barely conscious. "He's pretty drugged up and looked undernourished, but I think he'll be okay once we get him some help," said Alex. The car pulled around back and two men carried Carmen inside. Frank's heart pounded. His son was alive. He thought he would never see his son again. Frank called his personal physician and had him meet them at the funeral home. When the doctor arrived, Carmen was in the basement, on the same table that Johnny Rizzo, a.k.a. JR, had spent his last moments. Carmen was wrapped in blankets. "He looks dehydrated. Set up an IV," the doctor told the funeral director. He examined him as well as he could under the circumstances. "His heart sounds okay, but his blood pressure is low. I gave him a shot to put him to sleep. The IV should stabilize his condition and give him some nutrients. Let him rest for now. I'll stop by tomorrow afternoon and check on him," said the doctor. "Thank you, Doc, I owe you a great deal of gratitude for coming out so late. Please accept this gift for your services," Frank said as he handed the doctor an envelope. The doctor did not want to accept the cash, but knew it would be an insult not to accept it. Frank had been good to him.

"We need to get Carmen out of town as soon as he can be moved. The police will want to talk to him and the Bartello family will be gunning for him. If he all of a sudden shows up, there will be too many questions to answer. He needs to be somewhere safe till all this mess with the Bartello family, and all the dead bodies that keep showing up blows over. There's too much attention on the family now anyway. Alberto, make the arrangements," said Frank. How about our ranch in Colorado, it's desolate and easily protected?" Alberto suggested. "No," Frank retorted, "no place that the family has any connections or is associated with us. We can't take any chances. I don't want to lose him again. His mother, God rest her soul, would never forgive me," said Frank. "I promised his mother I'd take good care of him."

Bartello went nuts when Joey Pataglia told him about the raid on the town house. "Johnny Rizzo has disappeared too. No one has seen him in days. The Leones must have grabbed him and he ratted on us," said Joey. "But he didn't know that we had Carmen. Only a few people knew," ranted Bartello. "He did supply the drugs to our guards," replied Joey. "Maybe someone put two and two together, or one of our men was bought off, or they were followed. Although, the only ones who knew about Carmen are dead. One of them could have leaked it out," said Joey. "Well, if the Leones were behind it," Bartello said.

"Carmen will surface and we'll know. Call Garcia, I want him to be aware of any activity that involves the Leone organization. Frank has to be putting the pieces together and realizes we were behind both his son's and nephew's kidnappings. He probably realizes that Cortez was a pawn in the whole scheme and we used Cortez and his men to squeeze the Leone organization out of the market. I want a contract out on Carmen. This way we will know if he is around. It's all Frank's play now. My plan worked. We got rid of Cortez and helped Garcia establish. We crippled the Leone family and stopped them from increasing their drug trafficking. We control the drug market and Frank has to make a move if he wants to increase his market."

Carmen was ushered quietly and quickly out of town to a destination only Alex, Alberto, and Frank knew. Alex and Alberto personally escorted him. They were driving and would be gone for several days. They could not fly for fear of being recognized by the police or Bartello's associates. Carmen was well enough to make the trip. He would be in a safe environment. He would be staying at a private resort in the mountains and would be looked after by the owner, who was a friend of Frank's from their childhood days under the black hand. He would trust him with his own life. Frank had no vested interest in the resort, so no one would be able to trace it back to him. Carmen was instructed to blend in because he might be there for several months, or until it was safe to return.

CHAPTER TWENTY-SIX

David called Stone to tell him about Emily's decision to seek out the Leone family. "Do you have any other information I should know before I embark on this journey? I know it's going to be dicey. I can't stop her now," said David. Stone thought for a minute. David is in too deep. After all this time, the Leones would have made a connection with Emily. They have to know she is Sam's wife. They must know he is dead and don't want to draw attention. They may feel that it's better off him missing, than him turning up dead. They would have to try to explain the situation to everyone. "We discovered Frank's son Carmen hasn't been seen in a long time," Stone replied. Our contacts think he has come in harm's way also. There has to be a connection. I will tell you this much. Five members of the Bartello family were found dead in a condo in your town, near Riverside and Union several months ago. The police kept it quiet. Our people tell us it looked like a hit. Word on the street is there was bad blood between the families over drug control. We know there's been a few bodies turning up from both families. They won't have an all-out family war. That's not good for business. Be careful," said Stone.

Emily and David met at his office. They had to work out a strategy. She just couldn't show up on Frank Leone's door step asking questions. That would be the quickest way to be turned down. She needed to get close to him first. She knew Sam's parents were dead, he had told her that much. Frank would be the only person who would furnish any information. "How do we get to Frank? "We could follow him," suggested Emily. "That's a good way to get us both killed," responded David. "We need to set up an informal introduction from another avenue."

The Leone family had several legitimate businesses. One of them was a trucking and distribution center. David made several inquiries about the operation. They owned a fleet of fifty trucks and also leased out some of them. They contracted and shipped to mostly independently owned businesses. Frank made stops there at least once a week. He also had a nightclub on the downtown strip, where he spent most of his time in his office during the day. Maybe we could get an appointment with him posing as a potential small business owner who is looking for a receiving and shipping company, thought David. There's a sign on the trucks with the company number to call for information on shipping and delivering. He called and got an operator, who took information and told him that he would get a call back from their sales manager. He gave her his phone number, but changed the greeting to represent a specialized furniture dealer. He thought they may check him out, so he had Emily create a web site for "Specialized Home Furnishing," with his number and a fictitious email. He got a call back from the sales manager and arranged a meeting for the next afternoon. Emily left school early in order to make the two o'clock meeting." How do we get to Frank if we're meeting with their sales manager?" asked Emily.

"Good question, Emily. Let's play it by ear and hope we don't get one cut off if they find out we're lying. Did you check to see if we got any hits off our web site?" asked David.

"I did. We got three hits. I'm sure one of them was from Frank's company," said Emily.

When they drove up to the main gate, a guard asked for identification. David gave his own name and the guard checked his visitor's list. He opened the gate and motioned them to drive to the main entrance. The facility was large and about the size of a football field. They parked in front in one of the visitor's spaces. David noticed a large black sedan parked in the authorized parking only area. He hoped it might be Frank's. He took a deep breath. Emily looked nervous but determined. He opened the door for her and he followed her into the building. They were greeted by an attractive receptionist, professionally dressed in a dark grey business suit. There were three offices to the right and she led them to the farthest one. The office was impressive. It was well decorated with leather furniture. Two men stood up to meet them. One was average height, medium build and dressed in a suit and tie. He came from behind the large mahogany desk. The other man was well over six feet tall and had a slim, trim looking physique. He was very distinguished looking. His hair was a mixture of black and grey. He also wore a suit and tie and from what David could tell, a very expensive one. "I'm Tony Barone, the sales manager, and this is Frank Leone, the principle owner of our company." David almost fell over. What a stroke of luck. Emily was tongue tied for a minute. She was face-to-face with the man who could have all the answers. "I assume you're David Kimbro," continued Tony. "And who is this lovely lady with you?" he asked.

"This is my associate Amy Patton," replied David. Patton was Emily's maiden name. "Thank you for meeting with us. We are in the market for a carrier. Our business is starting to take off and we need the ability to ship in larger quantities and more often," said David. "Exactly what do you produce for transporting?" asked Frank. "We specialize in custom furniture," answered Emily. "We are actually a broker. We buy and sell" she said. Thank God Emily finally got her composure back, thought David. "Where do you normally ship to?" asked Frank.

David answered, "All over the country."

"Who have you been using?' asked Tony. Uh o, thought David. He wasn't prepared for that question. "FedEx," Emily answered.

"The problem is they charge too much for too little of a shipment. We need better pricing with larger shipping," she said.

Frank abruptly stood up and said, "Send us your itinerary, with shipping requirements and quantities per week and we'll work on a pricing structure for you. It is a pleasure to meet you both." Frank gave Emily a long, scrutinizing gaze as she stood up and walked out of the office.

"Wow," said David. "That was intimidating. Did you see the way Frank looked at you when we were leaving? Do you think he saw right through us?"

"I don't know. I never expected to meet Frank today," said Emily. "He is impressive. There is a resemblance to Sam. I couldn't help but feel Frank was going through the motions of meeting with us. Why do you think he was there? This was just an initial meeting that usually just the sales person would have, to gather information on a potential client. What do we do now? They called our bluff, asking for the breakdown of our make believe company?" asked Emily. "I don't know, like you, I never expected Frank to be there. At best I thought we would be able to find out when he's there. I don't like the feeling of this one" said David.

Frank watched David and Emily leave and drive away. He turned to Tony. "Get Alex and Alberto here as soon as possible," and he walked out of the office. He went out to his car to make a call. "I need you to send me all the information you can find on an Amy Patton. Patton may be her maiden name," said Frank. He walked back into the building to wait for Alex and Alberto. It was fortunate I was there today, he thought. Frank usually stops by later in the week. Thirty minutes later both men showed up. Frank asked Tony to leave so he could use his office to meet with Alex and Alberto. Tony closed the door as he left. "We got a problem. If I'm correct, I just had a meeting with Sam's wife. I've been waiting for her to surface," said Frank. Alex and Alberto had forgot about her. They knew he was married, but never met his wife. Sam kept her away from the family, just as he kept himself away. "Why do you think it's her?" Alberto asked.

"Years ago, Carmen wanted to reach out to Sam, but I advised him not to do so. Sam wanted no part of the family business, and I respected his decision. I secretly kept tabs on him and occasionally threw him some real estate deals, without his knowledge. Just wanted to make sure the kid was making his way. I have a picture taken of both of them shortly after they got married. I wasn't invited to the wedding, but I wanted a picture of my sister's son," explained Frank.

"Why didn't you ever show me?" asked Alberto. "She was my sister too!"

"I should have, but I was still upset that Sam avoided us. After we buried him, I got the picture out to remember him the way he was, rather than what he looked like when Alex brought his body home. When she came in today, it took me a little while to recognize her, but she is Sam's wife. She used the name Amy Patton. I already have someone researching that name. My bet is Patton is her maiden name. The guy she was with, I never saw before today. I think she is trying to make contact and find out if we know anything about Sam. Sam has been missing for months. She has probably been searching for him all this time, or any clues to his disappearance. Since we never met her, she probably feels we have information on him and she's coming to us," said Frank.

"How are we going to handle this?" Alberto asked. "Let's find out who this guy is she was with today. I don't think he is a cop. I called their bluff and asked for the breakdown of their business records and transactions in order to give them a cost from us. We have their picture on camera when they entered the gate. See what you can find out about them. This has to be very discreet. We don't want the police or the Bartello family finding her. They would use her against us like they did Sam," said Frank. The phone rang. It was the man Frank called earlier to find out who Amy Patton is. After listening for a few minutes, Frank said, "Just as I thought. Thanks for the fast response," and hung up the phone. Frank turned to Alex and Alberto. "She is Sam's wife. Our source identified Patton as Emily Carson's maiden name. Amy is her middle name. The man she is with is David Kimbro, a Private Eye. Apparently, she hired him to help her find Sam. A detective Becket was working the missing case, but cut her loose some time ago. He wrote it off as a disgruntled husband who fled the scene. It was a dead end for the police. They closed the case. I don't know how she found us. I guess the PI did his job. I don't know how we are going to keep a lid on this," said Frank. "She puts us all in jeopardy" commented Alberto. "If anyone should ever find out Sam is dead," said Frank, "we are all at risk. It would cause a lot of scrutiny by the police. We don't need anyone looking into our activities, especially now since Carmen is on hiatus. That would raise another issue. We should have dealt with her before this happened. I wonder why Bartello never used her?"

"Maybe he's waiting to see if she opens up a can of worms for us. This would take the pressure off of his operation for a while and keep us off balance," said Alex.

David called Stone. "Well, we met the infamous Frank Leone."

"Where and how?" asked Stone. "At his trucking business." David proceeded to tell him about the meeting. "You know the man's not stupid," retorted Stone. "You walking into his operation was a bold and dumb move. Do you think for one minute he doesn't know who his nephew is married to? If he hadn't reached out to her before, he must have a reason. He probably knows about Sam and does not want to tell her," said Stone. "Well, the next move is hers," said David. "He called her bluff."

Bartello had kept an eye on Emily as well. She was how he convinced Sam to participate in his plan to over throw Cortez's operation and to hurt the Leone family. He had threatened to torture and do unthinkable things to her if Sam did not cooperate. After all these months, Sam's body did not surface. Garcia left Sam's body at the Mexican factory for Leone to find, so they would think Cortez was responsible for his death. Whether they got it or not, he is not sure. Never a word on the street or from his associates. No police reports, or identifications were made from the mass graves the Mexican authorities found, nor whether they found Sam. He is sure that Leone's family made the hit on his condo and rescued Carmen. No word on Carmen's whereabouts. They must have stashed him somewhere. JR has vanished. He must have been the one who gave up the location. He is either long gone or dead. One of the men guarding Carmen must have opened his mouth. The men guarding Carmen were all long time, trusted members of the family organization. Bartello did not think any one of them directly betrayed him. One of them just made a mistake and probably slipped up and said the wrong thing to JR when picking up the weekly drug packet. JR was probably either paid well or tortured by the Leone family and gave up just enough information to find where Carmen was held. Bartello's guess is that JR has been at the bottom of the river. Bartello could not complain. His organization controlled the drug market and he was getting all the supply he needed at a great price, which was his reward for helping Garcia's cartel. It was now a waiting game. It's been a long time since all that happened. Sooner or later, Frank's family would make a move. Bartello thought about putting a hit on Frank. It would be risky and could start a war, but his organization would suffer the least since he controls the market. He has more men and connections. He generates more income for everyone by having an extended network of people depending on his operation. He has politicians, police, and judges, in his pocket and they are all aware of from whom they get their payoffs.

CHAPTER TWENTY-SEVEN

Frank left the club, as he usually does, before the night crowds start filing inside, he spends his evenings at home, watching all the shows he's taped, or reading a good book. His favorites are murder mysteries. He sometimes laughs out loud when he reads what some of the authors write about crime events that are extravagant and make them seem glorified. Crime should never be romanticized, it is a necessity and a way of life. His driver pulled onto the parkway, when a car pulled up beside them and suddenly fired three shots through the back window, striking Frank on the side of his head. Frank slumped in his seat. The car speed off as Frank's driver pulled to the side of the road. He panicked and jumped out of the car. He opened the back door and Frank slid out onto the pavement. The driver frantically waved for traffic to stop. He yelled for someone to call 911. He didn't know what to do to try to save Frank's life. He leaned over and cradled Frank in his arms and tears came to his eyes. This man he was holding has been a father to him. Traffic had stopped and people were running to see what happened. When they saw Frank bleeding from the head, they quickly withdrew. No one helped. They stood there staring. When the ambulance finally arrived, they pushed back the crowd and took Frank from his driver's arms. "He's still breathing. He has a weak pulse. Let's get him in the back and start an IV. Keep pressure on the wound. Let's get going to the Med if he has any chance of surviving," the EM said.

Alberto got the call at one thirty in the morning. Frank was at the Med, in critical condition in a guarded room. Alberto called

Alex and they both headed to the hospital. The woman who called was a nurse on duty in the emergency room. She recognized Frank and called Alberto. Her father worked for Alberto, driving a truck for their family trucking company. She said he had several gunshot wounds with one in the head. They brought him in about four hours ago. Alberto rushed into the hospital and the desk nurse directed him to the intensive care unit. Alex joined him shortly. It had to be an assassination attempt. Alberto told Alex, "Call some men to get here quickly. We need them stationed in the hallway and near the entrances and stairwells. If they find out he's still alive, they may come back to finish the job. Tell the rest of the family to stand down till we sort this all out. Don't let anyone do anything stupid until we can regroup. Our main concern now is to protect Frank. Keep everything going as if nothing happened. I'll handle the police and the media."

David turned on the news as he sipped his morning coffee. He almost dropped his cup. The news reporter was talking about Frank Leone. An attempt on his life, was what she said. "He is in intensive care on life support with what is alleged to be gunshot wounds to the head. No further information to report. We are waiting for a full report from the attending doctor. Rumors are flying that this was not a random shooting, but an assassination attempt. Police Chief McMurray will be holding a press conference at noon today to give an update on their investigation into this breaking story." David grabbed his phone and called Emily. He knew she would be at work, but he hoped she would answer. "David, I'm in a meeting with a parent, can I call you back?" she said. "Emily, Frank has been shot. I just heard the news report, an attempt was made on his life last night," David said.

"Frank Leone?" Emily asked in shock.

"Yes," he replied, "they think it was an assassination attempt. If it's true, you could be in danger. If a family war breaks out, you could be caught in the middle," David told her.

"Let me call you right back," she said. Emily got a sick feeling in the pit of her stomach. If Frank dies, I may never know the truth about Sam, she thought. Who knows that I am a family member of the Leones? Would anyone want to harm me to hurt the Leones? Did Frank's organized crime operations piss some other family off? She read about the Sicilian Mafioso and how they extracted revenge, but she thought those days were bygones. Why else would someone want Frank dead?

Bartello was relaxing at his office, reading the newspaper article about the attempt on Frank's life when he got a call from Joey Pataglia. "He's not dead. They didn't finish the job, but he is on life support. We can't get to him. The police have the hospital locked down. The Leones are there too. Everyone's on alert. If the Leone family reacts, we're ready," said Joey.

"Keep everything on a low profile. We don't want to scare any of our customers," said Bartello. Bartello was disappointed. If Frank was dead, it would be a quick ending. It may involve a small attempt at revenge from the rest of the Leone family, but without Frank's leadership, it could be over shortly. The family's power would break apart with no apparent heir, since Carmen was gone. But now, if Frank hangs in there, it would cause major problems. It would bring heat on Bartello for instigating such a move, and he knew it. Frank would garner a lot of sympathy from other families in other cities. A clean hit would be ignored most of the time as a business decision, but when you fail, it can only bring criticism.

Emily left her classroom and called David. "What now?" she asked. "I may never get answers. Who would want him dead?"

"I have a call to Stone to see if he can shed any light on the situation," replied David. "He told me before that there was bad blood with a rival organization. I have a call coming in know, I think it's him."

"Robert, what can you tell me about the hit on Frank Leone?" asked David. Stone replied, "The attempt was orchestrated by the Bartello family from what we hear. Probably revenge for the attack on their safe house a while back. Our main source of information comes from shared reports with the DEA. They have been watching both the Leone family and the Bartello family for a long time. There has been a new cartel out of Columbia, who the DEA believes is furnishing the Bartello family. They also think that Javier Cortez, leader of a cartel out of Mexico, was eliminated by the new cartel. Somehow, Frank's family was fingered for the dismantling of the Cortez operation, but the DEA doesn't think so. Right now, the DEA is integrating undercover agents into the cartel to learn their new transporting avenues. They know the Bartello family controls the drug flow and the Leone family has not been very active lately. Angelo Bartello is the big fish in the water we all want. Our combined efforts have not been able to get the break we need to nail him. He is well protected with many layers between him and his associates. We are also looking at some pretty high profile people he has in his pocket. We have to make the right connection or he'll walk. As usual, this is highly classified information, so if you get caught, take a cyanide pill."

"Very funny Robert, you know the information is safe with me. I owe you," said David.

CHAPTER TWENTY-EIGHT

David came around the corner, approaching Emily's house, when he noticed a car with two men across the street from Emily's house. Police or Bartello's men. Could be either one. David slowed down as he approached the car. He tried to call Emily to warn her about the men, but she was already coming down the stairs from her front porch. The two men burst out of their car and quickly approached her. David slammed on his brakes, jumped out of his car and ran up to the two men as they met Emily. One of the men turned to David and brandished his gun. "Stop right there." David froze. "We just want to talk to the lady," said the man with the gun. "What do you want?" asked a frighten Emily. "We have some information on your missing husband," he replied. "We need you to come with us."

"No way!" exclaimed David. "She doesn't have a choice. Now back off or you'll be riding in the trunk. Don't try to follow us," said the man as he pointed the gun at David's chest. David felt totally helpless. What had he let Emily get into? He backed off as the two men lead her to their car. As they drove off David memorized the license plate. He called Stone immediately. "What the hell David. I warned you to be careful. I'll run the plates and call you right back," said Stone." David got in his car and sat motionless. This is crazy. How could I let this happen? His phone rang. "Stolen plates, which is no surprise. We alerted the local police and our district office. They'll check for signs of the car you described on the intersection cameras, to see if we can get a direction point. Don't do anything foolish," Stone said.

Joey Pataglia sent his men to pick up Emily. His people had been watching her for a while. Ever since they snatched up Sam, they kept her under surveillance in case Sam was uncooperative. Now they needed her. With the failed assassination on Frank, they needed her for some leverage. She was the only one vulnerable, all the other family members of the Leone family were on alert. Joey knew that Sam was not part of the organization, so they knew she was not close to the Leones. Bartello had a plan to avert any retaliation from the Leone family. He would make her a deal. He wanted her to negotiate a peace between the families. In exchange for her cooperation, they would tell her what happened to her husband.

"Where are you taking me?" asked Emily. Neither man spoke as they headed to their destination. She was frightened. What do these men want with me? Are they with the Leone family? If they were, they would know I met Frank and am part of the family through marriage. If they were part of the police force, they would have identified themselves. *This could only end bad for me*, she thought. When they pulled up to the Labella Italian Restaurant, she was somewhat relieved. She was escorted to the back of the restaurant to a large, well-furnished office. A heavy set man, in an expensive suit and tie stood up from behind the desk to greet her. He introduced himself as Mr. Jones. "Emily Carson, it is so nice to meet you. Please have a seat. Make yourself comfortable. You're probably wondering why you're here. All in due time. Can we get you something to drink?" asked Mr. Jones. "No thank you. Am I you prisoner or your guest?" Emily asked curtly.

"You are here because we need your services," he replied. "We know you are a great teacher and work with children with disabilities. You must be a very patient and passionate person to be teaching these children. I have a situation that needs your skills. I also know you are Frank Leone's niece through marriage," he said. Wow, she thought, everyone knew this but me. "Who are you really?" she asked. "We heard about the attempt on your uncle's life," Mr. Jones continued. "We want Frank and his family to know that a certain family had nothing to do with it. They will want to blame an associate, which could result in a very messy situation. My associate would like you to assure the Leone family this family had no part in the shooting," he said.

"How do I do that? I don't have a relationship with the Leone family," Emily guardedly replied. "We know you met recently with Frank. We make it our business to know these things. All we are asking is for you to do some damage control, which would benefit both parties," he said.

"How do you propose I do this?" she asked.

"This is where your particular skills come in," answered Mr. Jones.

"What if I don't agree to do it?" she said.

"Then let me sweeten the pot. I can give you the information you have been seeking. I know what happened to your husband," he said.

Emily gasped. "How do you know?"

"That is irrelevant right now. Do you want to know?" he asked.

"Of course I do! I've' been waiting for a long time to find out," she said. "Then help us and you'll find the answers you have been looking for. But let me warn you, if you go to the authorities about our meeting, you will never know the answers, and someone else may be looking for you, understand?" he asked.

"Yes," replied Emily.

"We want you to visit Frank in the hospital and tell him we want to have a meeting with Alberto and Alex. We know Frank is incapacitated, so we want to meet with his top family officials. They will not meet with us without Frank's approval, this much we know. Tell him that we do not want a war. A war never has a winner. Both sides will suffer body and monetary losses. Do this for your husband. Also, do not tell your private eye either, and yes, we know about him too. Call this number when he agrees. Then we'll go from there," he said.

"Why don't you approach one of his family members or associates to do this?" she asked.

"We cannot get near any of them right now and besides, you are a neutral party and not a threat. His men would most likely react violently to any of our associates right now. When the meeting is over, I will give you the information you want," he said. "Give me some proof that you know where my husband is." Mr. Jones reached into his top-desk drawer. "I knew you would want some proof. Here is his business card and his car keys. Don't ask how we came across them." She looked at them in shock. This man was not lying. She was escorted out of the office and out of the back door to a waiting car. Not the same one that brought her here. They drove to her house. She went inside and looked out of the window to see if the men were still there. They were gone. She breathed a sigh of relief. She was sure they would be watching her every move. She wanted to call David.

CHAPTER TWENTY-NINE

Alberto was sitting outside the intensive care unit. The doctor had told the family about an hour ago what condition Frank was in: two bullet wounds in the right side of Frank's head and one in his neck. One was lodged in the back of the skull and the other one passed through his jaw and exited the other side of his head. The one in the neck passed also, missing his juggler by inches. He was stable and on a breathing machine. Despite all that, his heart is strong, thus giving him a fighting chance to survive. "He is in stable condition," said the doctor, "and does have brainstem functions. We aggressively resuscitated him when he arrived here, which gave us enough time to stop the bleeding. There is no evidence of an intracranial bleeding. We did a CT scan. The bullets did not damage any key blood vessels. The bullets missed the brain. We have maintained his blood pressure and oxygenation. The CT scan shows a bullet fragmentation in the back of the skull. We have to wait until he is a little stronger and see if we can or need to extract the bullet. He is very lucky to have survived. You may see him shortly, but keep it limited. He needs to rest," said the doctor. "Thank you, Doctor. I'll personally be here to watch over him and make sure he is not disturbed," said Alberto.

Carmen had become bored at the resort his father had him hidden away at. He enjoyed playing golf and his game vastly improved, but he missed the hustle and bustle of the family business. It's been months since he left home. He has had no contact with his friends or family. The only ones who know he is here are his dad and uncle, Alberto, who calls frequently to stay in touch. When Alberto called with the news of Frank's assassination attempt, Carmen went numb. He felt powerless. Here, he was tucked away from harm and his father winds up getting shot. "I should have been there, maybe this wouldn't have happened," said Carmen. He lost his mother, now he could lose his father. "Stay cool," Alberto said. "I'll make arrangements to bring you home. He is alive and conscious, but he's not out of the woods yet. He would not approve of you coming home yet, particularly with the recent events. The police are all over our operations. We don't need bodies turning up everywhere. I know I can't stop you from coming, but you must be discreet. Your popping up will draw attention. Just hold on and don't do anything stupid. I know your temper, but this is not the time to lose it."

Carmen hung up and threw his phone against the wall and knocked the lamp off the table.

David had been calling Emily's cell phone to no avail. He left her several messages. He called Stone to see if they had identified the car or a location where they may have taken her. "We have video of the car headed toward downtown. The last camera had them on McClain going toward Third Avenue. We lost them after that. There's no other street video cameras." Suddenly, David remembered, the Labella Italian Restaurant is on the corner of Third and McClain. Joey Pataglia owned the place and he is connected with the Bartello family. Maybe they knew who she was and were going to use her as leverage against the Leones. If they shot Frank, are they going after the whole family? She would be the most vulnerable, but how would they know about her, unless they were somehow tied to Sam's disappearance. "Robert, we have a major problem. I think the Bartello family took her. They must have found out she's related to the Leones." Just then David's phone rang. It was Emily. "Emily, are you okay?"

"Yes, but I am pretty shook up. Can you meet me at the park in twenty minutes and be careful you're not followed," and she hung up. He could tell by her voice that she was in some kind of danger. He drove around the block several times and backtracked to see if he was being followed. He knew how to recognize and shake a tail from his FBI days. Emily was sitting on the same bench they had sat on before, when they spent time together in the park. She embraced David and held on for several moments. He could feel her body trembling. "Did they hurt you?" David asked. "Not physically," she responded, "but they want me to set up a meeting with Frank's family. They did not identify themselves. A Mr. Jones did all the talking, he's the representative of some other group. He said they have information about Sam's whereabouts. He gave me these as proof." Emily pulled out Sam's business card and car keys. She sighed heavily. "I am to call this number when I get Leone's consent to the meeting. He claims that his group is suspected of orchestrating the hit on Frank, but that they are not involved. He wants to set things straight with the family."

"How do they expect you to do this?" asked David. "I don't know, but he did say if I want to know what happened to Sam, I would find a way to make it happen. He also said if I did not do it, I could wind up missing too and they know about you David. They know about you. Apparently we have been followed for quite a while. I was told not to tell you anything, but I had to. I can't do this alone." "It has to be a set up. Why don't they wait till Frank recovers? From what Stone tells me, the Leones have tightened their security on Frank and are keeping a low profile on their business operations. Bartello wants to hit them while they are vulnerable. Alberto is the family counselor and Alex is the under boss. Take them out now and Bartello's family controls everything. The Leone operations would crumble. Smart move on his part. We need to meet with Stone and plan your next move. I'm sure the FBI and the DEA would be very interested in the fact that the Bartello family reached out to you," said David.

CHAPTER THIRTY

Stone arranged a secret meeting with Emily and David. David picked Emily up after school. He feared her car probably had a tracking device. He gave his car a thorough inspection and came up clean. In case they were watching her at school, he went through several maneuvers to shake any tails. They met at an old office building that the FBI uses for storing surveillance equipment. Stone opened the door and motioned them in quickly. He had two cars outside on patrol for any intruders, just to be safe. "Follow me," he said. He led them to a small office with recording equipment sitting on a desk. "I would like to tape our meeting, if you don't mind, Mrs. Carson. I need every detail of the conversation with Mr. Jones." Emily agreed and proceeded to relay the whole conversation in detail. When she was finished, Stone asked her who else was at the meeting. He showed her a picture of Joey Pataglia. "I only saw the two men who brought me there, but I did see a figure in the corner. The light was dim but it could have been him. I can't say for sure," she said. Stone handed her three more photos. "Look at these three, do you recognize any of them?" he asked. She studied them for a moment and pointed to one and said, "That's Mr. Jones." Stone looked at David. "She just identified Angello Bartello. This may have been his first mistake, letting her see him. We could get him now for kidnapping, but it probably would not hold up. This is what we want to propose," said Stone. He turned to face Emily. "You're going to call Bartello and tell him you set up the meeting. He wants you at that meeting for assurance and probably to eliminate you also, as I am sure that's what he intends to do to the Leone representatives. We want you to be wired so we can hear the whole conversation and possibly get enough information that would get us an indictment. With both parties there, they are going to talk about their operations. Would you be willing to do this?" Stone asked. "How is this going to get me information about Sam?" Emily asked. "If I am right, it will come out during the meeting. One other thing, Carmen has been seen at the hospital visiting Frank. With him back, it could complicate Bartello's plans. We need to move quickly. Go to the hospital as a family member. My office will clear your visit with the police. Since Frank and Alberto already know who you are, tell them you were only seeking information about Sam. You didn't mean to deceive them, but you just recently found out about Sam's family. You just wanted an initial meeting to see who they were, with the intent to contact them later and identify yourself as Sam's wife. Play on their emotions. Then tell them about the predicament a man named Angello Bartello put you in when he reached out to you to try to set up a meeting to make amends with his organization. Tell them he said he contacted you because he could not make contact with any other family member. Tell them Bartello said his organization is not responsible for the attempt on Frank's life. Tell them he told me if I do this, he will tell me what happened to Sam. I would think that the Leones would also want that answer. We are placing you in a dangerous situation, the call is yours," said Stone. Emily looked David. He had been listening intently, but his face gave no trace of his feelings or opinion. He knew how important it was to her to finally reach the end of the road in her quest to find Sam. She turned back to Stone. "I'll do it. I'm scared, so let's do it as quickly as possible. I'll go to the hospital tomorrow," she said.

"You are a brave women. Why don't you stay at my place tonight? You need company and a cool glass of red wine. I have a bottle waiting to be opened," David said.

"I don't have any clothes, tooth brush, or any cosmetics," she said. "You can wear one of my shirts and I have extra tooth brushes. Tomorrow is Saturday, so you have no school. Let's get drunk and relax. I'll take you home tomorrow so you can go to the hospital to see Frank. Tonight, let's just enjoy each other's company," said

David. She was hit with two sensations. One of fear and one of lust. Could she contain herself, becoming this intimate with David? She was afraid if she had a couple glasses of wine she would be putty in his hands. She decided to throw caution to the wind and consented to spend the night at his apartment.

Carmen sat at his dad's side, holding his hand as Frank slept. He should have been here. He fought back tears, seeing his father laying here so vulnerable and weak. He was young when his mother died, so he grew up under the influence of his family. After college, he went right into the family business. He helped them improve their portfolio through wise business investments. He helped diversify the organization's holdings and make the organization legitimate. He was also very firm with the other family members and associates, and had a reputation for being violent when he didn't get his way. As a child, he was always getting into small scrapes with school mates and friends. If not for his father's position in the family, he probably would have been an enforcer for the organization. Now, all he could do was wait for his father to recover.

Emily parked her car and headed to the entrance of the hospital. She noticed two police cars parked beside the main doors. When she stepped off the elevator, she saw two policemen sitting by the doors to the intensive care unit. One of the men rose as she approached and asked for her identification. After checking it, he handed it back to her and opened the door to the IC waiting room. She saw three men sitting in the room. As she entered, one of the men stood up with a surprised look. He immediately recognized her. "What are you doing here?" he asked in a surprised voice. "I came to see Frank, my husband's uncle," she replied. So she knows, thought Alberto. Just then Carmen came out of Frank's room and Emily was shocked. For a fleeting moment she thought it was Sam. The resemblance was uncanny. He could be Sam's twin. "Who is this beautiful lady?" asked Carmen. She just stared at him, dumb founded. "She's your cousin in law," Alberto said. "She's Sam's wife." Alberto had previously told Carmen about what happened to Sam and that they buried him months ago. He regretted that they drifted apart after college and hadn't stayed in touch. He knew Sam got married, but Sam shied away from the family for years and did not invite any of the family to the wedding or ever introduced his wife. She was stunning. Carmen was always the ladies' man, and he knew Sam had good taste in women from their college days. "I am so glad to finally meet you. Sam and I were not only family members, but also close friends years ago. We kind of went our separate ways after college and lost contact with each other. He didn't want to work for the family business. He never was quite able to get his mind wrapped around our world. We handle business a little differently than most. What made you come to our family?" said Carmen. "I came to speak with Frank. I need his help," said Emily."

"We've met," said Alberto. "What do you need to speak to Frank about?" asked Alberto. "I need his help to find Sam." All the Leones looked at one another. No one spoke. "Why come to us after all this time?' asked Alberto. "I only recently found out about Sam's family. He never spoke of you. It was almost as though he had no family. I just attributed it to his having a dysfunctional childhood that he did not want to talk about. I figured one day he'd tell me about his upbringing. I gave him his space," she explained. "Do you think we know anything about Sam? We have not had any contact with him in years. Why are you looking for him? Are you still married?" Alberto asked. "Yes," replied Emily. "He disappeared six months ago. The police filed a missing report, but gave up, figuring he ran off with another woman. I don't believe that's what happened. They closed the files. There was no indication that he intended to leave me. Everything he owns is still at our home or in his office. I hired an investigator who I passed off as my associate when we met at your trucking firm. The trail we followed, lead to a man called Mr. Jones and a man named Joey Pataglia. Sam was last seen at his real estate office after the night he met a client at the Labella Italian Restaurant," she said. Alberto, Alex, and Carmen listened intently. "Mr. Jones, who my investigator believes is Angello Bartello, had his men take me to the restaurant and asked me to help them in exchange for information on Sam. That's why I'm here. To discuss it with Frank," she said. "Exactly what is it? Frank is in no condition to discuss any proposals," said Alberto. "Bartello wants me to arrange a meeting for him with you and Alex to clear the air. He insists that I be present also. He claims he had nothing to do with the attempt on Frank's life," she said. Alberto just stared at Emily. Carmen went to say something, but Alberto motioned for him to stay silent. Carmen had a history of over reacting. "Why do you think he wants this meeting?" Alberto asked. "I don't know" she said. "He did say that if there was any retaliation on your part it would be hurt both organizations. It would be bad for business. That's all I know."

"It's a trap," chimed in Alex.

Alberto cast him a stern look. "When does he want this meeting?" asked Alberto.

"As soon as possible," she replied.

"How do you contact him?" asked Alberto.

"He gave me a number to call," she replied.

"Give me a number to reach you," said Alberto. Emily left the hospital, feeling that the Leones were not telling her something. They didn't flinch when she told them Sam was missing.

Carmen was the first to speak. "It's a set up!" he exclaimed. "You're right," said Alberto. "It's a smart move on Bartello's part. Eliminating Alex and me would vastly weaken the family. He knows we suspect him of Frank's attack. With Frank neutralized, and us out of the way, gives him the perfect opportunity to dissolve our organization. He has always wanted Frank's politicians and judges in his pocket. A complete take over. We can't burden Frank with this situation now. Sam's wife being present gives Bartello the assurance that the meeting would be considered peaceful on our part. He's drawing us into his web," said Alberto.

Emily called David and told him about the meeting at the hospital. "I never got to talk to Frank. Sam's uncle Alberto did all the talking for the family. Somehow I have a feeling they know something about Sam. They never reacted when I told them Sam has been missing. Can I come over? I need company," she said.

CHAPTER THIRTY-ONE

Alberto called Emily the next morning. "Set up the meeting. Tell him to meet us at two o'clock at our trucking company's parking lot. It will be outside in public, where everyone will feel safe. Meet us there at one thirty. Don't bring your PI. Come alone. We will prep you for the meeting."

"I'll do it," Emily said. Emily called the number she had from Bartello and relayed the message. "Alberto said to meet at their trucking company's lot. He wants it outside in public so there are no surprises. I'll be there as you requested. Will you give me the information I want then?" asked Emily. Bartello's mind was racing. He needed to get set up quickly and have his men in place. Alberto would already have his men strategically placed around the building. He would rather have a different location to meet, but he had to take advantage of them agreeing to meet at all. He was familiar with the area. There were several warehouses adjacent to the trucking company where he could station some of his men. He only needed a clear shot to take Alberto out. If he got Alex, all the better. He knew this was a risky plan. Once the shooting started, he would bolt for his car and speed away, hopefully catching the Leones off guard. "I'll be there," answered Bartello. "If all goes well, I will provide you with the answers you seek."

David listened to Emily's and Bartello's conversation. He immediately called Stone. "It's on. The meeting is set up for two o'clock at Leone's trucking company. Where should we meet you?" asked David. "The same place we met before, within the hour. We don't have much time to prepare her. Make sure you are not followed," said Stone.

David was a nervous wreck. He could only imagine how Emily felt. When they arrived at the FBI warehouse, David turned to Emily and said, "Are you sure you want to do this? It's not too late to back out. You're putting yourself in real danger."

"I have to see this through. I need the answers for me to move forward with my life," said Emily. They went inside where Stone and three of his men were waiting. "Emily, take off your blouse. George is going to put a recording device on you. It is very small but very powerful. I doubt that anyone will search or look for one since you will all be outside and both families will not suspect either party of wearing wires. We will be able to listen and record anything within twenty feet from you. Our men will be stationed nearby. If you are in danger at any time, just say, "It looks like rain," and we will move in to rescue you. It is overcast, so they should not suspect anything until we move in. If all goes well, just leave and we will take over from there. Drive to this building. We will meet you here. Just act as natural as you can. Any question?" asked Stone. David pulled Emily aside and held her hands. Stone and his men left the room. David looked at her, then leaned into her and gave her a long, passionate kiss. She wanted to leave and go back to his place, but if she didn't see this through, her life would never be safe, not to mention never knowing about Sam.

Emily drove into the parking lot at exactly one thirty. Alberto and Alex were waiting for her. "Park over there," Alex said. She didn't see any other cars in the lot except one, which she assumed was theirs. "We think this is a setup. We have men concealed in and around the building. We want Bartello to expose his hand, but not before we find out his motive. We want him to talk about his proposal and what he plans to do to keep the peace. Buy time. We have to wait for him to make his move," said Alex. Alberto came over and asked her how she was doing. "Very nervous, I just want this over with," she replied. "You're a brave women. Sam would be proud of you," Alberto said. She was startled. What did that mean, Sam would be, as in the past tense. *Was Sam already dead and they know this? Why won't they tell me? Am I being used by the family to extract their revenge?* thought Emily. Just then the Bartello family arrived. She had to regain her composure. They were early, probably to catch the Leones off guard. Two black Lincolns pulled into the lot and circled around to face the entrance. This maneuver did not escape Alberto and Alex's attention. Two men stepped out of the car and looked around. The driver opened the back and Angelo Bartello emerged and stood there as Alberto approached him. Bartello extended his hand to greet him. "I am so sorry to hear of your brother's condition, I've been praying for his recovery. I want to assure you that my family had absolutely no part in this travesty. We want peace between the families. We are business people," said Bartello. "Are you willing to share the drug market which you have so conveniently taken control of since a new cartel has established itself in the city? This would be in good faith to show you are serious about maintaining the peace," said Alberto.

"Your brother is a smart businessman," replied Bartello. "Word on the street was that he was striking a deal with Javier Cortez, a cartel leader out of Mexico, who I read was gunned down at one of his distribution centers. He was our supplier. I heard from my Mexican contacts that his whole manufacturing plant was raided, leaving the place a bloody mess. The police found bodies in a mass grave not too far from the plant. Whoever put the hit on him slowed down the traffic flow. Your family was trying to gain a larger share of the market. This would have cut into my territory," continued Bartello, "but I never complained. I knew it was business. You have a number of judges and politicians in your pocket. If we shared our drug territory, we would like to have access to your connections when needed."

"Your drug business never missed a beat from what we have witnessed," said Alberto. "Who is your drug supplier now?" asked Alberto. "Not until we reach an understanding," replied Bartello. "I'll have to meet with the family to discuss your proposal," said Alberto.

"Don't wait too long. This offer is on the table for a short time. It's being done to show good faith between families and to insure the peace," said Bartello. Alberto looked Bartello directly in the eyes and asked, "What do you know of my nephew's disappearance?"

"Which one?" asked Bartello. Emily's heart raced. "How did you know there was more than one missing?" Alberto questioned him. Bartello caught himself, "I meant which one of your nephews was missing, was there more than one?" he asked coyly as he glanced at Emily. If she had a gun she would have shot him on the spot. He is toying with us, she thought. Alberto asked again, "Do you have any information on Sam or Carmen Leone?"

"No, I don't, replied Bartello." He again shifted his eyes to Emily. Did she tell them I had information on her husband? Emily stared back at him. "Thank you for meeting with me. Call me at this number," said Bartello as he handed Alberto a card. He turned and walked to his car and glanced at Emily one more time. He decided to wait and not make the aggressive move now. Before I eliminate them all, I want to have possession of all the Leone family's connections. When they take the deal and give me what I want, and we set up the exchange, then, I will eliminate them all.

Emily turned to Alberto as Bartello and his men drove off. "What the hell was that all about? Did you already know Sam was missing? Did you see him look at me when you asked him about Sam? He's going to think I told you he had information about Sam. Now, he may not share anything with me for fear it would implicate him in Sam's disappearance," said Emily. Alex and Alberto looked at each other. "Come into the office. We need to tell you something," Alberto said with a stern face. Emily froze. *Oh my god*, she thought. *They know what happened to Sam.* Her knees got weak. She was not prepared for this. She followed them into the building and went in the back office where she first met with him and Frank. "Have a seat on the couch. Would you like something to drink?" asked Alberto.

"No," she replied, "and I would prefer to stand."

"As you wish. What I am about to tell you could cost you your life. We did not reach out to you before in order to protect you. We know where Sam is. He was kidnapped, we believe by the Bartello organization, and was held hostage for leverage against us. Frank was in the process of increasing our market in a business deal that had its operation in Mexico. As you heard, it would have cut into the Bartello organization's territory. Carmen was to go to Mexico as the family representative to observe the operation and report back to us before we consummated the deal. The day Carmen was to leave for Mexico, Bartello's family kidnapped him and held him also. Sam and Carmen, as you saw are dead ringers for each other. We assume they wanted Sam to take Carmen's place and they must have persuaded him go there to disrupt the negotiations. They knew Sam could pass as Carmen. They probably threatened Sam and programmed him to pass as Carmen. This is the part where I think you should sit," said Alberto. Emily collapsed on the couch. "We sent a team to the Mexican facility, in search of Carmen, when we had not heard from him. Alex led the team. When they arrived at the facility, they found blood and debris everywhere, but no bodies. Someone had taken the bodies, but did not clean up. At first there was no sign of Carmen. When they searched the building, they found a locked room in the back. When they opened the door, they found who they thought was Carmen in a vegetated state. He had been tortured and was dehydrated. He had obviously been denied food and water. We brought him home, but he was already gone." She gasped then sobbed as Alberto continued. "When he was taken to our family's funeral home, Frank discovered that the body was not Carmen. We had our medical connection run a DNA test on the body and found out it was Sam. "Oh my god!" Emily shouted. "He had nothing to do with your family business, but he died being part of what he never wanted!" she exclaimed.

"We are so sorry that Sam was dragged into this mess," Alberto said, trying to comfort her. "They also held Carmen, but fortunately we were able to rescue him. He was in bad shape when we found him. You saw him at the hospital and can see the resemblance to Sam. We felt the best way to keep you safe was not to involve you till everything settled. I know it had to be torture not knowing where Sam was. We did not think the Bartello family would use you, let alone know you existed," said Alberto. Wiping tears from her eyes, Emily responded, "I want to be part of the plan to take down Angelo Bartello and I may have a way to accomplish this," said Emily.

Emily drove back to meet David and Stone at the FBI building. She was careful not to be followed. "Did you get enough on

Bartello?" she asked Stone. "No, we need something that directly ties Bartello to a crime. If he admits a hit, or a drug deal, or bribing an official, then we can take him down. All we have right now is his admission to knowing information about a drug cartel and Frank's business. He never admitted he operates a drug supply operation," said Stone. "Well, I have a way to get you that information, but it has to be on my terms," Emily said. "Let's hear it," replied Stone. "First hear me out, I can get the Leone family, Alberto Leone and Alex Leone, to arrange a meeting with Bartello. Bartello wants what they have as you heard, on tape. The Leones will discuss the drug trafficking details. Bartello will have to divulge his involvement, in order to meet the demands of the Leone family. He wants the Leones' legal and political connections, and the Leones will make him identify his, in order for both groups to share. The catch is, the Leone family is exonerated out of the conversation and no admittances or statements will be used against them," she said. Stone was shocked. He hesitated for several minutes. "Do you want the big fish or not?" Emily asked sarcastically. "You can get the Leones to agree to this?" asked Stone. "Under these terms and a signed document of all the conditions I just stated from the DA's office. You see, they have a vested interest in this. I lost a husband and they lost a family member," she said. "Let me run this by the DA's office," said Stone. Emily replied. "Make it quick before the deal goes away and the Leones take matters into their own hands."

David drove as Emily sat in silence. She was still in shock finding out her husband was gone. She thought he may be, but the realization now made her feel empty. He must have suffered terribly, she thought. Maybe I should have pushed him more to talk about his family and at least had a relationship with them, that possibly could have avoided him being so unprepared for such a travesty. Maybe I can help avenge his death. His family is probably not much different, but I was married to one of them. "How are you holding up?" asked David. Now that she knew, hopefully she will move on, he thought. "I'll let you know when the score is settled. Right now, I need a long, hot bath and a good night's rest. I have to go to work tomorrow Please drop me at my house," said Emily.

David dropped Emily off and called Stone on his way home. "What do you think?" he asked.

"David, I told you awhile ago what you were getting into. I am still in shock. Her proposal is unheard of. To exonerate one crime group to prosecute another is unusual. The fact that the Leone family agreed amazes me. I will call the attorney general's office tomorrow. This is a little above the local DA's spectrum."

CHAPTER THIRTY-TWO

Alberto, Carmen, and Alex sat in the office reviewing the meeting. "She is brilliant," said Carmen. "Her proposal would put the Bartello family in a heap of trouble. It would take them out of action for a long time, even if they never got fully indicted. During the time it would take to investigate them and bring them to trial, which could be long, they would be crippled. Their entire organization would be under extreme scrutiny. All their connections would go into hiding. It would take the heat off us. We could operate behind the scenes, and recoup all we lost to Bartello. It doesn't fully avenge Sam, but it will be nice to see Bartello squirm under the pressure from the Grand Jury," said Carmen. "The problem with all this is we expose our family business," commented Alberto. "Even if they agree not to incriminate us, they would have information they could use to come at us another way later. We have to make the decision. Frank is not in any position to process the situation. Let's wait and see if the feds go for the deal," said Alberto.

Sam was dead. The peace of knowing was outweighed by the sadness that she'd never see him again. He was a good, hard working man, who tried to notch out his own place in the business world. He helped everyone he could to realize the America dream of owning their own home. He sacrificed commissions and his time to make deals work. Even though the romance and passion had dwindled, and they drifted apart, she still loved him and probably always would. Ten years of marriage would do that to a person. Due to this, she will help avenge him one way or another. She couldn't tell anyone about Sam without raising all kinds of questions. He was buried in an unmarked grave for now, by the Leone family. For the time being, it was better left he was still missing. Alberto said when this was over he would take her to his grave site. He said that it may have to be that Sam remains missing forever. Trying to explain his death would incriminate everyone and subject the family to intensive investigations and expose all their business operations. For now, she would have to accept what Alberto said.

CHAPTER THIRTY-THREE

Stone called the state general attorney's office the next morning. Jason White was a friend of Stone's. They worked a few cases when Jason was in the district's DA's office before he became the state attorney general. White had given Stone his private cell phone number. White answered on the second ring. "Robert, how are you? I doubt this is social call. Am I right?"

"You are and how are you? I need to meet with you on a very sensitive matter, the sooner the better," said Stone.

"This sounds very serious," replied White. "How about ten tomorrow morning, in my office. I gather this is an FBI confidential issue?" asked White.

"Yes, it is, and that would be great. I know you're busy, so I'll see you tomorrow. Thanks, Jason." Stone hung up and called George, a specialist for the FBI in communication and tactical surveillance who would be needed to set up the necessary equipment. He would need George to verify the taped meeting of the two families.

Stone and George walked into White's office. Jason stood up and shook Stone's hand. Stone introduced George. White gestured for the two men to sit down. "Well, what is so important to bring you to my office?" asked White. Stone proceeded to tell him the whole series of events involving the Bartello family and the Leone family. He told him about Emily's involvement and the circumstances regarding her dead husband. George played the tape and White listen intently. "You realize the tape is not specific enough to use against either family?" asked White. "I do, but if we make the deal that Emily proposes, we could get Bartello to incriminate himself. I know it's out of the box, but we haven't had anything good to nail Bartello with. We've been watching him for a long time and this could be the break we need," said Stone. "She has you sold on this?" asked White. "You are asking us to turn our backs on the Leone family to nail Bartello? What do we do with the dirt on the Leones? Forget it exists? Do we erase the part where the Leones incriminate themselves? So we give immunity to them in exchange for them becoming informers?" asked White. "Yeah," said Stone. "Something like that." White sat motionless. This is incredible, he thought. One crime organization drawing out information from another crime family on tape for the FBI to use to convict said party. A boss of a crime organization wearing a wire to incriminate another boss. "My concern is if we prosecute one crime organization, do we leave an opportunity for the Leones to strengthen their position and take over Bartello's operation? How does this benefit our position? You know someone will step up to take their place," said White. "Not if we put pressure on the people who have been taking payoffs. All their names should be revealed and we will have them on tape. Even the Leones won't be able to use them again. We agreed to only grant immunity to the Leone family, and no one else," said Stone. "Do they know they may have to testify, even if granted immunity, or they could face charges?" asked White.

"Yes, they have a good family lawyer. They want it in the documentation that they do not have to testify," Stone said. "Give me a day to run it by the DA," White replied.

"Jason, we don't have much of a window," Stone said. "With Frank lying in the hospital, the family is making plans to protect their interests and won't wait long. Also, we need to keep Emily on board. This whole deal is predicated on their trust that she can make it happen. She is the connection and the contact between us. She is the one who convinced them to make a deal. It's a good plan for them and us."

"I'll see what I can do," said White. "I'll call you." George and Stone left White's office and headed back to the FBI office.

David thought he would give Emily some time to process the news that Sam was dead. He knew she was preparing herself for this outcome, but finally knowing someone is gone is always hard. He was sitting in his office when his phone rang. It was Emily. "Hi David, I don't want to be alone any more. Can I come over?"

"I'm at the office. I'll meet you at my apartment. We can go out to eat or we can order in."

"I don't feel like going anywhere. I just need to be comforted. I'm tired and glad that it is finally over, may Sam rest in peace. I'll see you shortly."

Emily left her house and didn't notice the black sedan following her. She stopped at a red light and a man approached her car. She recognized him as one of Bartello's bodyguards. He motioned for her to roll down the window and he told her to pull over after the light changed. She pulled over and parked and Bartello's car pulled in front and stopped. His guard opened her door and asked very politely to join Mr. Bartello in his car. She hesitated and his man assured her that Mr. Bartello only wanted a minute of her time. She sat next to him in the back seat. "I wanted to thank you for arranging the meeting the other day. There has been enough bloodshed as you heard at the meeting. The Leones have agreed to the terms we set forth at the meeting and we are in the process of determining a neutral location to finalize our negotiations. I want you at that meeting. I am not an unreasonable man. I will provide you details that you would not hear from anyone else. It will provide you with the answers you seek. However, with you present, it assures me that the Leone family will not pull any funny business. I will contact you where and when it takes place. Have a nice day Mrs. Carson."

Emily was a little shaken when she arrived at David's apartment. He noticed it immediately. "Are you all right?" he asked. "I was just stopped by Bartello and his men on the way over. He thanked me for the meeting between the families. He also said he wants me at the final meeting. Apparently, the Leones have contacted him and agreed to the terms set forth by Bartello."

"Stone never called me to confirm the DA's office accepted the deal," said David. "I wonder if the Leones are going to make a move on their own."

"He also said that he had detailed information on Sam's situation, that the Leones would never share with me. If they act without the FBI involved, how safe will I be?"

"The Leones will never allow you to be present," said David. "They couldn't take a chance that you could be wired or provide vital information on their operation that could be used against them without the guarantee of immunity. The DA's office needs to act now. I'm calling Stone and telling l him they moved up the meeting. It's now or never if the FBI wants any chance to take down either family." David called and had to leave a message. It was late in the day and Stone probably was at dinner or in a meeting.

Stone got off his call to his counterpart in the DEA and saw that David had called and left a message. Oh shit, he thought, this is going too fast. Why are the Leones pressing? If the DA agrees, this could be a sweet deal for them. There must be another agenda. He called Jason White. "We need to move now. I just got word the Leones are setting up their own meeting without us. Angelo Bartello contacted Emily Carson and told her that the Leones accepted the terms between the families and he wants her there for added assurance that the Leones won't lay a trap. The Leones won't want her there for fear she could be privileged to incriminating evidence that could be used against them. Even though she is family, they know she could be working with us. They won't take that chance, unless we can get the go ahead on the deal she arranged for the Leones with us. We need that paper work documenting their immunity," said Stone.

"I don't think that's going to happen," responded White. "It's a hard sell giving immunity to a whole organized crime family."

"Well, the blood bath that's coming is on the DA's hands," said Stone.

Stone hung up and called David. "I can't get the deal, the DA's office won't approve it. I guess we need to brace ourselves for what's coming. Emily's in a real bind. If the Leones don't want her there, and the Bartello's do, the meeting may never happen. This could leave Emily out to dry and endanger her life. She already knows too much for either side to want her around. I'm sorry David, there is nothing I can do, as much as I would like to bring both families down."

CHAPTER THIRTY-FOUR

Frank was slowly healing, but still in intensive care. Alberto was in charge now and he had to make a decision for the family on making a deal with the DA. The more Alberto thought about it, the deal would expose them and they would lose their valued connections. Without them, it would seriously affect their entire operation. They were valuable pieces of the structure an organization needs to survive. It was protection needed to conceal and abate any legal ramifications. We have to deal with Bartello's family ourselves, in our own way. He was well protected, especially since his attempt on Frank's life failed. We need to get next to him or find his weakness. Alex was sitting across from him, watching Alberto in deep concentration. "You're right, Uncle Al," Alex said after Alberto shared his thoughts. "We need to take down Bartello ourselves. I have an idea. The one person we know who can get next to him is Sam's wife, Emily. He's met with her and wanted her at our meeting, probably as a protective measure. He's holding information about Sam over her head. He doesn't know we already told her, and we all know Bartello was responsible for Sam's death. What if we had her set up a meeting with him and she delivers her own vengeance?"

"What are you suggesting?" Alberto asked as he stared at Alex in disbelief.

"I'm just saying," suggested Alex, "she could deliver the knock-out blow that we aren't in a position to do. She has as much, if not more incentive, than we do to avenge Sam. The question is how much and how far she would go?"

"How do you propose she does this?" asked Alberto.

"They'll search her for any wires and weapons. They know she is part of our family. They won't trust her. Bartello is only using her to get to us," said Alberto. "Exactly, that's why she could pull it off. They would never suspect her. She would catch them completely off guard. We get her to set up a meeting and we provide her with the method to kill him."

"Assuming she would agree to this," Alberto stated," what weapon could she use? We know they'll search her."

"I realize that," said Alex. What does every women with long hair use to keep their hair back? A hairpin. A very long and sharp hairpin. They would never see it," said Alex. "Yes," said Alberto, "but she would have to be precise in delivering the strike. It has to be perfect. If she fails, she's dead. What about anyone else being in the room with them? She needs an escape route."

"She would need a distraction," explained Alex, "in order to get his men away from them and occupied for a few minutes. The best place for them to meet would be at Joey Pataglia's Italian restaurant, Labella's. It's a public place and Bartello will feel comfortable. We could create a diversion, long enough for her to act. She would then walk out the front door before anyone knows what happened. We pick her up. We'll be gone before they know he's dead."

"Great plan," replied Alberto, "but there's still the problem of getting Emily to agree to do this. It's a very big deal, you know, to kill someone, no matter who they are."

"I agree, Uncle Al, it's a long shot, but we have no other options right now. The longer we wait, it places Frank in grave danger. You know Bartello will make another attempt on Frank, before he fully recovers. He can't afford not to. He will strike while Frank and the family are weak."

"This is crazy," said Alberto. "All we can do is ask her and play on her sympathy for Sam. Remember, she said she wanted to be part of the plan to take Bartello down," replied Alex.

David told Emily what Stone had said. She was visibly upset. "What's wrong with them? We hand them the Bartello operation on a platter. I'm the one taking a risk. I can't believe they won't make the deal. Stone said they wanted Bartello for a long time."

David said, "They don't want to give the Leone family immunity."

"So they want to have their cake and eat it too," replied Emily. "They're willing to let Bartello continue, when they could get overwhelming evidence against him? Would not at least bringing down one crime operation be worth it? Sam died for nothing!" she exclaimed. David saw a side of Emily he hadn't seen before; pure hate and bitterness. He was now worried she might do something rash. Her life was in danger, because she knew too much about both family operations. They would all be watching her closely. David reached out and hugged her as she sobbed in frustration.

Alberto's sedan pulled up to the front of Emily's school building. Classes were just starting to let out. A few minutes later, Emily came walking out with two of her fellow teachers. Alberto stepped out of the car. She glanced over and saw him. Her heart raced. What now? She hadn't expected to hear from him, now that the deal was off the table. She excused herself from her friends and approached Alberto. "What do you want now? I can't help you," she said in a low voice so her friends couldn't hear. "Do you remember when you said you wanted to be part of the plan to take down your husband's killers? Do you still feel that way?" Alberto asked. Emily thought for a minute. "How can I help?" she asked. "Give me twenty minutes of your time, and I'll explain." Emily got in the car and they drove away.

She sat on the couch in the office of the delivery Express Trucking Company. Alberto sat behind the desk and folded his hands. He looked Emily directly in the eyes. "We feel the loss of a loved one, just as you have. We were not close to Sam over the last ten or so years, but we kept track of his business activities. Frank threw a lot of business Sam's way, unbeknown to him. He is our sister's son, which makes him a blood relation. We saw him grow up as a member of the family. He and Carmen were once inseparable. Sam did not want to work for the family, which we all respected. It did not mean he was no longer a family member. Bartello tried to use him against our family. Sam died a hero. Whatever they tried to accomplish with

139

him, we may never know. He was an innocent victim who died a tragic death. Bartello needs to pay for these transgressions. We have a plan to do just that. It involves you. You are the only one who can get close enough to him to inflict damage."

"What kind of damage?" asked Emily.

"Permanent damage," replied Alberto. She looked over at Alex and Carmen, who were sitting behind her with serious expressions on their faces.

She turned back to Alberto. "Are you asking me to murder Bartello?" she asked, raising her voice in disbelief.

"Yes, we are," replied Alberto. "But hear me out. Before you say yes or no, this is something you will have to live with for the rest of your life, just as you have to live with the loss of Sam. Killing someone is not easy, but sometimes it needs to be done. Your life will never be safe. You know and heard too much at the last meeting with Bartello. We can't protect you forever, neither can your private investigator friend. In fact, they may go after him, knowing you employed him and confided in him. If there were another way, we haven't found one. No one is safe; not you, your friend, Frank, no one associated with our family. We are all at risk unless Bartello is eliminated. "How can you put this responsibility on my back? I'm just a schoolteacher, not an assassin. I don't know how to kill someone. This is absurd!" exclaimed Emily. She stood up shaking. She couldn't believe what she just heard. "I know I just upset you," Alberto said. "But you have to realize what's at stake here. If you want a future, this must be done. We will train you on what to do. We will have your back through the whole process," he said.

"Process, is that what you view as killing someone!" shouted Emily. She sat back down and tried to wrap her mind around what had just been proposed. "Now I realize why Sam never wanted to be part of his own family," she said. "That why Sam needs to be avenged. He wasn't part of the operation, by his choice, yet he died because of who he was," answered Alberto. She sat in silence. "Can I get you a drink?" asked Alex. She looked at him and realized how easy these men took murder as a way of life, as if a drink could wipe away any guilt feelings or remorse. This is everyday business to them.

She hesitated for a long moment before saying, "If I do this, it would only be for my husband. I want his grave site to be marked with the proper monument he deserves. If I am killed in the process, I want to be buried next to him."

"This we can do," said Alberto.

Emily was driven back to her car at the school. It was getting late and she was tired and hungry. As she drove she kept going over and over in her mind the conversation she had with Alberto and Alex replayed in her head. It seemed like a bad dream. It was almost a hopeless case. If she complied to kill Bartello, could she live with this? If she didn't, it would be just a matter of time before she met the same fate as Sam, at the hands of the Bartello family. She couldn't tell the only person she trusted, David. He would try to talk her out of it, but he couldn't assure her safety either. It was scary. Her weapon would be a long, thin hairpin, long enough to inflict death when punctured properly. She would have to get close enough to him to deliver the strike. His eyes were the perfect target, Alex said. Drive it into his eye as far as possible, and it will puncture the brain. Instant death would occur. Then turn and walk out to the waiting car.

She was to call Bartello and ask for a private meeting as the go between him and the Leones. She would tell him she wanted to meet at the Labella Italian Restaurant at his office so they could both feel safe. They were to discuss the information that would be exchanged between the families and set up a final date and meeting place. In good faith, she was to ask for him to send his men to pick her up at her home. That way, she wouldn't have to worry about her car after the hit. This is a long shot. What if she fumbles and misses his eyes? The phone rang. It was David. She hadn't called him for fear she would give in and tell him about what the Leones proposed. She so wanted to tell him and somehow have his support, but she knew better. "Can I come over?" he asked. "I've had a rough day and I have two parent meetings to prepare for tomorrow," she said. "I'll call you after the meetings." She needed time to wrap her mind around the evening's events. She needed to look long and hard into her soul to determine if she could do such a thing as murder.

CHAPTER THIRTY-FIVE

Emily was jolted from her sleep by the blaring of her alarm clock. She slowly rolled over to see what time it was: 5:30. She hadn't slept much that night as she thought about the events of the previous day, but she'd finally been able to get to sleep at 3:00 a.m. If only she could call in sick to work today, but she'd already used up all her vacation days. She reluctantly got out of bed, undressed, and stepped into the shower. She drank a cup of black coffee as she put on her makeup. She couldn't concentrate on her parent meeting preparation. All she could think about was Bartello's eyes. She kept thinking of different ways that she could get close enough to stab him in his eyes. She had to get close to him, enough to feel his last breath on her face. Her face flushed and her hands shook. She knew prayer would do no good. God would never approve. She was on her own on this one. She had to justify it in her mind. An eye for an eye. How apropos that is. She went into the closet and stroked Sam's clothes. She needed to feel his presence to commit this act. Would he approve? She doubted it, but if their places were changed, he would kill in an instant to keep her safe. She decided to go through with it. It had to be right away, before she changed her mind. She would call Alberto today and tell him she'd set up the meeting with Bartello this week.

Emily called the number Alberto gave her from the card Bartello gave him. "Mr. Bartello, this is Emily Carson."

"I was expecting your call," said Bartello. "Alberto told me you would be acting as the liaison for the Leone family."

"I would like to meet with you to firm up the exact terms and establish a meeting time and location for the exchange of information. The Leones would feel much better if I set it up, acting as a neutral party. Since I am not involved in the family organization, which you are well aware of, I am intervening as a communication source for both families. Remember, you wanted me involved in making these arrangements. It was you who requested me taking a part in the first place. When can we meet?" she asked. Bartello hesitated. "Where do you suggest we meet?" he replied. "How about Labella on your territory. I do have one request. Can you have your men pick me up?"

"Agreed," commented Bartello. I'll have my men pick you up tomorrow night at seven o'clock." Emily hung up and collapsed on her couch. It was done.

Emily called Alberto. "It's all set. Tomorrow night his men are picking me up at seven. We'll meet at the restaurant. Make your preparations and please don't fail me."

"We won't, just walk out the back door. A car will be waiting. It's going to get bloody. We have to make sure we eliminate anyone who sees you at the restaurant, so tell his driver to take you through the back entrance. Tell them you don't want anyone in the dining area to see you. The meeting is to be private. We'll take care of the rest. If things go badly, run. We'll have the place covered. Remember, don't hesitate. Get it done quickly."

Now she was a nervous wreck. It was about to happen. Her hands shook and her knees felt weak. She poured herself a tall glass of wine. She wanted to see David. It could be the last time if things went badly. She started to pour her second glass when the phone rang. She looked at her caller ID. It was David. She quickly picked up the phone. Desperate to hear his voice, "David, I'm so glad you called. Can you come over?" she asked. "You sound worried, is everything all right?" he asked. "It will be as soon as you get here. Bring your tooth brush and a change of clothes. You're mine for the night."

Emily spent the evening with David as if it would be her last. He was overwhelmed with her affection. Was it just lust or pent up emotions over the last year, caused by stress and loneliness? He sensed something was weighing heavily on her. All he could get out of her was her need for him to comfort her. He would enjoy the moment and hoped that it would develop into a long term relationship. She was the most gentle, caring person he had ever met. She was laid back and always looked on the bright side of things. Her personality was infectious. However, tonight he felt a different vibe. She's been worried, depressed, and stressed. Something was consuming her and at the same time distracting her. Maybe it was the let down and the finalization that the whole situation was over. Little did he know what was in store for her and the chance she would take to avenge and protect herself. He fell asleep with her in his arms.

Emily could hardly concentrate the next day at school. All she could think about was what would take place this evening. Her nerves settled a little bit, but she knew that they would get worse as the appointed time arrived. Maybe two glasses of wine, but no, that was just for entertainment. She needed her head straight. The day dragged on as she went through the motions of teaching her class. When school let out and the last student was put on the bus, she headed for the door. She didn't speak to anyone and drove straight home. She sat down and wrote David a letter in case she didn't make it, thanking him for his help and friendship. She wanted more from him and she wanted to let him know how much she'd grown to care for him. It was lust, passion, and love, all wrapped in one. She wished she had met him sooner, meaning no disrespect to Sam. Sam was older than her and was set in his ways. He did not possess the passionate spirit that David had. David could be the serious experienced lover she needed, fulfilling all her desires. She finished the letter and placed it on her kitchen table. She didn't feel like eating, so she showered, dressed, and sat in her living room waiting for the hour to approach.

CHAPTER THIRTY-SIX

It was seven o'clock when she heard a car in her drive way. She looked out and saw the black sedan she had come to know so well. As she exited her front door the driver got out and opened the car passenger door for her. They drove in silence. Her hand kept touching her hair, feeling the long hairpin. She prayed it would do the job. Alex showed her how to inject the pin quickly and with force. Here she was about to commit a murder and she was praying that she could do it right. What did God think of her now? She had to think of something else or she would change her mind. This man had to die. He exemplified evil. How many had he killed or had ordered killed? She knew of a least one; her Sam. She would concentrate on this thought as she proceeded with her mission. The car pulled up to the back entrance as Emily had requested. Joey Pataglia met her at the door and escorted her to the restaurant office where Angelo Bartello was waiting. The guard at the office door patted her down as Bartello apologized for the inconvenience, but said it was necessary under the circumstances. "She's clean," said the guard. "Come in and make yourself comfortable. Can we get you a drink?" asked Bartello. "Yes, please, a seven and seven would do, thank you." She needed a stronger drink, but it would throw off her concentration. She felt her nerves again, being so close to the action she would take. Hopefully, a drink would calm her down. She glanced around the room. Besides Bartello and Pataglia, two other men stood in the back. She sat across the desk from Bartello. The guard handed her the drink she asked for and also handed Bartello and Pataglia one. Bartello had asked for scotch and Pataglia, a rum, and coke. "Let's talk a minute about your association with your family. I am led to believe you haven't had much contact with the Leone family these last ten years or so. How is it that they trust you to be their representative for such delicate negotiations?" asked Bartello. "I thought it was more by your request that I am involved in this situation," she replied. "True, I feel less threatened with you being the one to be the go between. Besides, I have something you want, so I know you will be wanting the arrangements to be settled quickly."

"When are you going to tell me about my husband?" asked Emily. "I'm here and have done what you have asked, so tell me now. You once told me you would in due time. The time is now, so tell me," she said. She watched him shift in his chair. He was weighing if he should wait till after their meeting for the arrangements to be determined or tell her now and take the chance of alienating her before the deal was finalized. "Let's discuss the terms of the deal. The Leone family will divulge all their political connections and make them available to us. In return, we turn over part of our drug operation territory and introduce them to our supplier. Is this agreeable to them?" asked Bartello. "Yes, this is what they stated to me. Plain and simple. They also want a guarantee that no more attempts will be made on Frank's life. They are not accusing your family, but feel you have enough influence with other associations to put out the word to refrain from doing any harm to Frank or any of the Leone family." Although, she and the Leone family knew it was Bartello who ordered the hit on Frank. "This deal requires good faith and effort to make it work," she continued. "Now what about Sam?" She wanted to hear the lies from him so she could reaffirm her desire to kill him. "Your husband was in the wrong place at the wrong time. We believe his own family had him involved in negotiations for a big drug transaction. Our informers have indicated to us the deal went bad and your husband got caught in the cross fire. He was collateral damage, used as a pawn by the Leones to secure a drug cartel operation. Probably a little out of his expertise, being a real estate broker." She wanted to climb over his desk and attack him right now. This just made her job all the easier. "Did anyone ever find his where-abouts or see his body?" she asked.

"I don't know," answered Bartello. "Maybe your husband's family knows that answer. That's all I have for you. Now, let's figure out a place safe for both parties to meet and exchange our information. She glanced at her watch. Alberto told her that he would give her thirty minutes before he created a diversion. She had five minutes to make her move. "Why don't you come and sit beside me, while we decide on a meeting place. I feel like I'm in school talking to my principal with you sitting behind your desk. I could use another drink, if you don't mind," she said.

"Get the young lady another drink and one for me also," Bartello said as he moved to the couch to sit next to Emily. He sat down and placed a hand on her knee. "You are a very attractive lady. It is unfortunate that your husband can no longer enjoy your lovely company," he said as he stared into her eyes. Unbelievable, she thought, he was trying to charm me. This made it easier to get him close. Just then, a loud noise came from outside the office. It sounded like a big commotion. Two loud bangs came from the restaurant. One of Bartello's men came rushing into the office to tell him that a car had been driven through the front window of the restaurant by what appeared to be a drunk driver. "I'll handle this," said Pataglia, "Come with me," he told the guards. They left the office and Bartello turned back to face Emily. She plunged the metal hairpin deep into his eye socket with all her force. He was startled. He reached for his eye to try to pull the pin out. He fell forward and was dead before he hit the floor. Emily stood up and watched as he slouched in a heap. She was successful, the pin had penetrated the brain. She wished he had suffered more. She regained her senses and ran from the office to the back door. She heard gun shots and glass breaking as she opened the door and jumped into the waiting car. Alberto was in the back seat next to her and grabbed her hand. "Did you get the job done?" he asked. She shook her head yes and Alberto squeezed her hand. "Relax, it's over. You are safe now and no one will be a threat to you." They drove off in the night as she sat in silence. She was numb.

They dropped her off at her house. She was trying to digest what she had just done. She slumped on her couch, exhausted and horrified. She questioned her own self-worth, killing a human being. She would forever try to justify her actions. Her phone rang and startled her out of her trance. "Emily, I've been calling you. Did you see the news?" David asked. "No, I just walked in," replied Emily. "Where were you? Turn on your TV. It's all over the news." She turned on her television and saw Labella Restaurant. The front of the restaurant was smashed in and the back of a car was protruding from where a large window had been. In the upper corner was a picture of Angello Bartello. "Someone hit Bartello at his restaurant," said David. "Bartello's dead! They haven't said how or who killed him. Joey Pataglia was also murdered along with three of their men. I tried to warn Stone. The Leones must have acted on their own. "Emily dropped the phone and burst out in tears. David could hear her deep sobs of pain. "Emily!" David shouted. "What's wrong? I'm coming right over."

She slumped back on her couch and cried deep, painful, sobs of grief. Reality was sinking in. Seeing is believing, and there it was, right in front of her face. The picture of a man she murdered. She took a life and that bell could never be unrung. Five men died tonight because of her. She sat there mourning their deaths when she heard a pounding on the front door. She jumped up and immediately thought the police were here to take her away. A chill went down her back. "Emily!" David shouted, "Are you in there? Open the door." She opened the door and threw herself into David's arms. He held her as she wailed deep moans of despair. She was crying uncontrollably. Just short of being hysterical. What had happened, he wondered. What catastrophe could have brought this on? Then it hit him like a ton of bricks. She must have been at the scene in the restaurant when the murders occurred. The Leones had used her to set up this assassination of the Bartello family bosses. That's why she didn't answer her phone. "Tell me Emily," he demanded "What did you do? Did you take part in the hits at the restaurant?" She couldn't answer, she had no control of her emotions. She just kept crying. He held her tightly. Was he about to lose the best thing that's ever happened to him? How deeply is she involved in this mess and what part did she play? What kind of retaliation was coming her way? When she finally settles down, he hoped he would get some answers out of her. For now, he just held her and tried to comfort her.

"Do you think Emily's okay?" asked Alberto.

"I think she is," Alex answered Alberto. "She was quiet on the ride to her house. She did a magnificent job. Sam can rest easy now. He has been avenged. Now we have to tell Frank. He won't be happy that we involved Emily."

"Let me worry about that," said Alberto. "Our whole family and our operations will be under heavy scrutiny, so we have to be careful. No one can identify any of our family or associates to tie into the hit. We can't reach out to Emily either. We don't want to lead anyone to her. With both Bartello and Pataglia dead, their operations are weak and will probably lose many of their contacts. Everyone will go into hiding, including us. We have to take a low profile on all our activities until this blows over," said Alberto. "Don't forget what we promised Emily," said Alex.

"I know," said Alberto, "but it will have to wait for a while. We'll get a message to her. Let her know when the time is right. We'll take her to Sam."

CHAPTER THIRTY-SEVEN

Stone called David the next morning. "Did you know about the hit on Bartello?"

"No, I knew nothing about it, but you remember, I suspected something was going to happen. I warned you. You guys should have made the deal. Now all you have are a bunch of dead bodies with probably more to come," said David.

"One good thing," commented Stone. "This wipes out the Bartello family power. At least for a while."

"Any idea who pulled off the hit?" asked David.

"Probably the Leone family for retaliation for Frank," said Stone.

"I realize that, but do you have any idea who actually killed Bartello?" asked David.

"The initial report was he was killed with a metal pin forced through his left eye that pierced the brain. Someone had to be real close to pull that off. It had to be someone he trusted to have that close to him. Probably an inside job. One of his trusted men may have betrayed him. But what puzzles me is why they didn't just shoot him. Why a metal object through the eye? Any of his men would all have a piece on them, unless he was with someone who did not want to appear to have a weapon. Someone outside the family, who they would search before letting them get close to Bartello. He was killed in the office of the restaurant. They found him on the floor. Someone killed him while a battle was going on in the front section of the restaurant. They must have exited through the back entrance," said Stone. David felt a cold chill run through his body. Stone was possibly describing an outsider who wanted revenge. Someone who could catch Bartello off guard. Someone he knew who posed no threat, like a pretty lady schoolteacher. A metal pin would be undetected, hidden in her hair. The Leones must have come up with this plan. They played on Emily's emotions. "Were there any witnesses?" asked David. "None that are alive that we know of," said Stone. "The dead were all identified as Bartello's men. There was so much damage to the front of the restaurant, it almost appeared it could have been a distraction. The patrons and all the help ran out the front when the shit hit the fan. Pataglia and all the others were found dead in the restaurant. Only Bartello was in the office. Whoever killed him was alone with him and fled quickly."

"Did you find any prints on the weapon?" asked David. "No, the blood from his brain washed off any evidence when the coroner extracted the pin. It was jammed in so far, it stopped at the back of his skull. The final push was probably done with the palm of the hand. The head of the pin was very small. The pin was four inches in length. A good clean hit. No bleeding out. No messy evidence. He died instantly, according to the coroner's report. The assailant wouldn't have any blood or DNA on their clothing. Like I said, a good clean hit. A professional most likely, hired by the Leones." Stone paused for a moment. "How is Emily doing?" David almost detected a note of suspicion in Stone's voice. "She's fine. A little upset over the whole ordeal," he replied. Stone's too smart not to start putting things together. If Emily had anything to do with Bartello's murder, he would flush her out. "Well, keep me updated," asked David, "if you don't mind. I guess I can close my case and move on." He hung up and walked back into Emily's bedroom. She was sleeping. She finally stopped her crying after exhausting herself and fell into a deep sleep. He stared at her for a long time trying to recreate in his mind what could have taken place with her ending a man's life. For now he slumped in a chair and watched her sleep.

CHAPTER THIRTY-EIGHT

Frank was steadily improving. His condition was upgraded to serious. He remained in the intensive care unit, mostly for observation. The internal bleeding had stopped and he was conscious and breathing on his own. Alberto sat by his side and quietly brought Frank up to date, being careful to leave out anything he felt would upset Frank. He told him Bartello and Pataglia are dead, but not who did it. He told Frank he was now avenged and was safe from any assassination attempts. When they move Frank to a private room, Alberto said he would bring him up to speed on all the events that occurred since he has been in the hospital.

A week went by with nothing new in the news about the death of Bartello and his men. Frank was released from the hospital and was resting at home. Emily was back in her classroom, still upset over the recent occurrences. She waited word from Alberto about visiting Sam's grave. She knew David suspected something, but he was giving her some space. She knew she would have to tell him everything eventually but didn't know how or when. She wasn't so sure how he would react, but to have a relationship, she'd have to be completely honest. They had continued to see each other, but she could tell David was not completely relaxed. It was almost as if he were waiting for the truth to come out. She didn't even worry about the police or anyone else finding out she was the assassin. If she told David, maybe he could help relieve some of her guilt. He, above all, would understand her actions. Would he support her? She wasn't sure if he could accept the fact she killed someone, still be able to love her, and want to spend the rest of their lives together. She went over and over in her mind the night of the murder. She was hoping it would make it seem as a bad dream and not reality.

Alberto and Alex were sitting with Frank in his bedroom. "I've seen the news. One of you tell me that one of our men killed Bartello. If it was, how come he didn't use a gun and how did he get close enough to stab him in the eyes?" Alberto and Alex looked at each other. "Alberto spoke first. "Emily did it." Frank glared at him in dismay. "You involved her in murder!" Frank shouted. "We had no choice," said Alex. "He already had a hit on you and we knew it was just a matter of time till he finished the job. We had to do something to protect the family. He got what he deserved. She was our only option to get close to him. She did it willingly." "Is there any chance it could be traced back to her?" asked Frank. "No, it was a clean hit and a clean getaway. She went in the back door to meet him and the only ones who saw her were Bartello's men, and they are all dead. She went out the same way. Alberto was in the back waiting for her. We created a distraction so she could be alone with him. It was over in a matter of minutes. Me and our men cleaned up the mess up front. No one else saw her come or leave. Not even our own men knew she was in the office with Bartello. She had his driver pick her up and deliver her to the rear entrance. The driver was eliminated too. No one knows but us three what really happened. There's no way she could be connected to the murders."

"What about the private eye she had working with her? They seemed more than just business acquaintances," asked Frank. "We figured that," said Alberto. "They have been spending a lot of time together. I'm sure it's more than a business relationship. Emily's a beautiful women and Sam's been gone a long time. I guess she needed someone for company and anything else. I think we should thank her for taking out Bartello. Help her to start a new life. Relocate her. We could arrange for that. Set up an account with enough money for her to start over. We owe Sam that much." Frank thought about it for a second. "Get in touch with her," he said. "Very discreetly. We don't want to draw any attention to her. Arrange a meeting for her to come here. Make sure no one sees her. I want to talk with her."

"Frank, we also promised her we would take her to Sam's grave so she could say her goodbyes. She also wanted a proper head stone. We told her he was in an unmarked grave, in order to conceal his death from the authorities. Maybe we could take her there now," said Alberto.

CHAPTER THIRTY-NINE

David sat across from Emily in their favorite pizza restaurant. She picked at her slice of pizza and sipped her glass of beer. "Emily, I need to know what you've been keeping from me. You can't let a door stand between us. If you want to continue a relationship, you have to be honest with me." She looked at him and smiled. She had fallen in love with him. Sam was a good provider, dependable, straight laced, and very practical. David was kind, gentle, compassionate, a great lover, and a very good listener. She was also afraid she would lose him if he knew the truth. "Not now," she said. "We'll talk back at my house." She knew she had to tell him. It might as well be tonight, she thought. If he rejected her, that would be two men she lost within a year.

Emily poured David and herself a glass of wine. She needed a little help to tell him the whole story. They sat in her living room and drank their wine. She wanted to finish at least one glass before she began. It relaxed her and hopefully relaxed him in preparation for what was to come. "The Leones wanted to set up a meeting even before the DA's office turned down the deal. They knew it wouldn't be accepted. They contacted Bartello and said they wanted to meet and try to work out what both families wanted from each other. They felt that Bartello would make another run at Frank and they wanted to insure the peace between the families. However, the Leones knew that Bartello would set a trap and the Leones would be walking into it. They had to get to him first. Bartello fell right into their plan. Bartello wanted me to set up the arrangements for the terms and the meeting place. Bartello felt if I were there, then the Leones would not plan any retaliation of their own. Alberto and Alex Leone approached me to first meet with Bartello as their representative to go over the terms and location so there would be no misunderstanding when they met. It was then, that Alex informed me that they intended to kill Bartello." David was on the edge of his seat. "They told you this?" he said in disbelief. *Yes!* His mind was slowly confirming what he thought.

She continued, "They laid out a plan. I was the only one who could get close to Bartello." She took a drink and sat back. That explains the hairpin. He thought for a quick second that maybe someone else delivered the death blow and she just carried the weapon into the meeting. He prayed that's what happened. "I was there, David. I am responsible for the death of Angelo Bartello and everyone else who died that night. I struck the blow that killed Bartello." David suspected she did it after learning the facts from Stone. He hoped he was wrong, but here she is admitting to the crime. "How did you escape? There were no witnesses," he asked in amazement. "I went out the back door and Alberto drove me home. I'm not sorry that Bartello is dead. I wish I didn't have to be the one to end his life. I am going to have to live with this. He was an evil man and that made it that much easier to do. Part of me wanted revenge and part of me just wanted to get on with my life. I knew I couldn't do the latter with him still around." David stood and said he needed another drink. She poured them another glass of wine and sat down. She tried to gauge David's feelings. He was staring at her. She couldn't tell if he was disappointed or disillusioned. "I am truly sorry I took a man's life. As I said I will always regret what I did and tried to justify it, but in the end I acted out of hate, frustration, and revenge. I can't unring that bell. If you hate me for being part of this, I understand. I love you very much David." She broke out in tears. "Emily, my sweet Emily, I love you too." He held her tightly and wiped away her tears. He knew he could never leave her.

Emily went to school the next day feeling better since she told David. They spent the night together just holding each other till they fell asleep. They didn't need to talk. They were now bound together by a secret. Her day was the usual chaotic cycle dealing with highly autistic kids, demanding her time and attention. The day goes fast under these circumstances and there never seems to be enough time for her to do all her lessons and paper work. She walked out of the building at the end of the day exhausted and saw a strange sedan with tainted windows parked next to her. As she approached the vehicle, the back window rolled down and Alex stuck his head out. She stopped. "Hi Emily, I didn't mean to startle you. Frank would like to meet with you. He's at home now doing much better."

"I didn't think we would have contact for a while," she said. "You did want to visit Sam's grave site? We can arrange it. Frank would like to see you first. Can you come now? He is expecting you." He stepped out and opened the door for her to get in. She hesitated, but felt she wasn't in any danger. If they wanted to hurt her, they could have done that the night of the murders. They would have reason to do it then, eliminate her and all evidence of her, and any chance she could connect them to the killings. "How have you been?" asked Alex. "Considering with what happened, I'm still sane. My job keeps me occupied."

"You'll adjust," he said. "It takes a while to get over something like this. It's never easy. Hopefully you'll come to realize it was for the best. Your life would never be safe otherwise. I know you miss Sam. We all wish we had had a relationship with him and got to know him. His mother was my aunt, as you probably know. I wasn't around her much, but my dad and uncles used to talk about her a lot. She was the youngest sister of the family. Frank can show you pictures of Sam's mom and dad."

"That would be nice" she replied. They were silent the rest of the ride.

CHAPTER FORTY

They pulled up to the gated entrance at Frank's house. A large man was at the gate and waved them through. They pulled up to the house and the driver opened her door. Frank's home was gigantic. Beautiful, sculpted columns. Large glass windows and a double, stained glass door adorned the front of the house. Marble stairs lead up to the front door. It looked like a palace. Alberto was there to greet her. "Please come in Emily. This is your home also. You are part of the family. What's ours is yours. We are so glad to see you and delighted you came. Follow me to the study. Frank is there relaxing and waiting for you." Frank was sitting in a lounge chair in a cotton robe. He looked better than she anticipated considering what he went through. "Emily, I am sorry I can't get up to greet you. I don't have all my strength back yet. You look lovely. Would you like something to drink?" he asked.

"No, thanks, why am I here?" she asked abruptly. "Please have a seat. First, I want to apologize. I recently found out what you went through for the family," he said. "I am so sorry that these idiots involved you in such a sticky mess. It took a lot of courage to do what you did. We are eternally grateful. I'm sure Sam was very proud of you." He hesitated and tried to gauge her mood. She sat staring at him. He continued, "Alberto told me of your desire to visit where Sam is buried. We can do that, but to move him or mark his grave would raise a lot of issues, mostly by the authorities. How could we explain his death without implicating ourselves? It's best he remains missing. We know what you've been through." He hesitated again, watching her reactions. "We have a proposition for you." Oh no, she panicked. "I'll take that drink now," she said in a shaky voice. "Relax Emily, it's not what you think. We think it would be in the best interest for all of us, if you took an extended leave, and left town. You have a good excuse, having lost your husband. You need time to get away from all this and get your life back together. We have set up an account for you with a large sum of money to finance anywhere you want to go."

"I don't need your money," she interrupted. "I can make it on my own."

"Please let me explain," he continued. "There has been a trust fund established years ago for all the family children. We didn't forget Sam. This money now belongs to you. We want the best for you Emily. You have an opportunity to start over." She sat back in her chair to process what he said. "What if I ever want to come back?" she asked. "We hope you will someday, but not for a while. It takes you out of sight and out from under any scrutiny from outside sources. When it all blows over and everything gets back to normal, maybe then. For now, you need to disappear." He quickly recanted, "Bad choice of words, I apologize."

Emily thought about Frank's proposal. She knew it was the right move. She was a nervous wreck waiting for the next shoe to fall. Maybe a change of scenery would be good and relieve the pressure. Out of sight, out of mind. The old saying could work in her favor. The trust fund Frank gave her was a small fortune. She could retire now if she managed her expenses properly. If she sold her house, she would net a nice profit also. However, teaching is in her blood, so she knew retirement wasn't an option. Her biggest problem would be David. How would she tell him? Would he be willing to go with her? Could she even ask him to?

After she decided to accept Frank's offer, she knew she had to talk to David. She invited him over for dinner. They could not talk in public about such a delicate situation. He drove up and knocked on her door. She opened the door, grabbed him, pulled him close, and held him for several minutes. This can't be good, thought David. "Something's wrong! I can tell," he said. "After dinner," she responded.

"I want to discuss something with you, but it can wait till we eat." David sat at the table and Emily served dinner and poured them each a glass of wine. They didn't have much conversation as they finished their meal. Emily cleaned the table while David poured another glass of wine. They moved to the living room and sat facing each other. "David, I have to make a very important decision. I had a visit with Frank Leone. Before you come unglued, let me explain. I never told them about you. They don't know that I told you anything. They know we have some sort of relationship, but that's it. I would never put you in danger. The Leones would like me to go away for a while. There is no way that the police can connect me to the murders, but with me not around, they think the police will not even consider me. No one saw me but I think the Leones are worried I could suffer from remorse and cause suspicion."

"What are you telling me Emily, are you thinking of leaving?"

"I have to consider it under the circumstances. I don't know if I can continue like this, as if nothing happened. The only good thing that's happened through this whole affair is finding you. I love you David. I need you to help me put the pieces of my life back together. I don't want to start my life over without you. It's not fair to ask you to come with me."

"It sounds like you already made up your mind to leave," he said. "Yes, but not without you." David knew it was the smart thing to do. Even he worried she would yield under the pressure of guilt. He would rather she move than lose her to prison. "Don't say anything now. Just think about what I just said." She leaned over and kissed him, then stood up and led him to her bedroom.

David left Emily's house in the morning and drove to his office. He wanted to call Stone and get a feel for the situation and find out if there was anything new. He thought about her protection. Should he go with her or remain behind in order to stay on top of the investigation by the FBI? Stone was no dummy. If he ever connected the dots, it's all over. He already is thinking a women may have committed the murder. If he left town with her, it could raise a lot of suspicion. Stone answered as usual on the second ring. "Robert, any news on the Bartello murder?" asked David.

"I was about to call you," said Stone. "Forensic found a trace of skin on the pin head. It came off the killer when they applied the pressure to enter the brain. It's a small sample that is referred to as touch DNA. Touch DNA samples are processed exactly the same way as blood, semen, saliva and are admissible in court. Humans shed thousands of skin cells every day. The cells are transferred to every surface our skin contacts. If the killer left a sufficient number of skin cells on an item at the crime scene, it can be collected as possible evidence. However, since touch DNA is usually deposited in smaller amounts than blood or saliva, it's harder to obtain DNA profiles from touch DNA samples. We don't know if they can use it to find enough DNA. They'll run it through the data base and see if anything comes up." David's heart sank. He was reminded, there is no such thing as a perfect murder. "Still no witnesses?" he asked. "No, we are still canvassing the area, and questioning the employees to see if anyone is holding any information back, either out of fear or being an accomplice. The funny thing is Sam Leone has still not turned up. We think maybe he's dead and Bartello had something to do with that also. It makes sense, Sam Leone missing and Frank Leone almost assassinated. The two are somehow tied together. It had to be Bartello's doing and the Leones struck back. We do have DNA on the Leone family. Some of their members have records. We'll find out. How is your client holding up? Does she still believe her husband will show up one way or another?" asked Stone. "She's doing okay. I think she has come to the realization that he is never coming back. She is thinking of getting away for a while," David said. He waited to hear Stone's reaction. "We'll, I'm sure you will keep track of her in case he does surface, dead or alive."

Emily's not out of the woods yet, thought David. After his conversation with Stone, he was praying that there was not enough cells to provide evidence. He wasn't worried about the Leones. If they did have enough skin cells to make a DNA match, it wouldn't be a Leone. She wasn't a blood relative. If they determined that it didn't match a Leone, they would look elsewhere. This goes back to making Emily vulnerable. Stone would realize Emily had a motive. If he ever found out, would he thank her or arrest her? David couldn't imagine

Emily not in his life. He never married and was tired of in and out relationships. One man's loss is another's gain, as the saying goes. It is unfortunate for Sam to not be able to live with Emily forever. He didn't think Sam appreciated what he had in Emily. He was sure Sam meant her no disrespect, but he didn't cherish the time he had with her. Maybe not having any children separated their relationship. Sam was an only child, so he may not have put much stock in having a family. Emily, on the other hand, loved children. You could see it in her passion for teaching. She is still young enough to start a family. I could see myself with her raising a few kids, he thought. Now, that may never happen. She plans to leave and I can't blame her. She wants to distance herself as far as possible from this mess. She's scared and torn about leaving and losing what we have. The Leone family will always be a reminder of what she did. They want her to leave for their own selfish reasons. She is the only one who could bring them down for all the other murders that happened that dreadful night. She could get immunity if she testified against them, but he knew she would never do that. They were Sam's family, and she once loved him. She also knew they could be as treacherous as the Bartello family. It would be a no win for her. He knew her best scenario was to get as far away from the situation as possible. He loved her, but he had to let her go. He would wait for her. When things cleared up and she was no longer living a nightmare, she would come back to him.

After their meeting with Emily, Alberto asked Frank, "Can we trust her not to crumble under pressure? She could sell us out if it came down to it. I'm too old to go to prison. Even if we send her away there is no assurance that she would remain silent."

"Don't forget Alberto," said Frank, "she would be incriminating herself. She did come through for us and herself, but I understand your implications."

"Frank," Alex said, "Alberto's got a point. We would always have this hanging over our heads. She's the only one who can tie us to the killings. She could make a deal. After all, Sam's dead, so what loyalty or connection does she have to us? We should have left her at the scene after she killed Bartello."

"You mean kill her then and leave her body?" asked Frank. "You guys are the ones who involved her in the first place. I would never have approved such a bold, stupid move. If she disappears now, it would certainly arouse suspicion. It has to look like she left of her own accord."

"So you're considering the fact that she is a liability," said Alex. "What about her boyfriend, how much does he know?" asked Alex. "This thing just keeps snowballing," replied Frank. "Remember Frank, she is not family blood. We didn't even know her till recently. We don't know what she is capable of doing. Sam's wife or not, she could ruin us all," said Alex.

Emily realized the possibility that the Leones would not just let her walk away with everything she knows. Their offer was an attempt to either buy her or get rid of her. After she called and accepted their deal, she asked for them to take her to Sam's grave. They agreed and said they would call her with the appropriate time. Alberto said they could lock up all the financial arrangements then and grant her access to Sam's trust fund. She couldn't help but feel an uneasiness in his tone of voice. Was she reading too much into it? Her intuition told her differently. She called David. She needed his input. She couldn't shake the feeling she was being set up. They wouldn't harm her here in town. It would raise too much attention. If they had a plan, she would meet her fate somewhere else.

CHAPTER FORTY-ONE

Emily met David at his apartment. She wasn't sure if her house was being watched. The fact that the Leones made an offer for her to leave town, meant they considered her a liability. She could end up like Sam. Would the nightmare ever end? Once she got in bed with the Leones and committed the crime, it started a flood of repercussions. She knew the Leones were no different than the Bartello family and every bit capable of doing anything to protect their interests. She wasn't a blood relation and they didn't know her before this happened. She would just be collateral damage to them. David met her at the door. "I'm glad you came. We have to talk. About the other night, I need to tell you how I feel," he said. "David, I need your help," she blurted out. "I think the Leones are going to eliminate me. I just have a bad feeling about the arrangements they presented to me. I think they want to shut me up permanently. If I leave town, I will become alone and I think they will act then. It would be too risky to try anything here." David put both hands on her shoulders. "I have to tell you about my conversation with Stone first. They found traces of DNA on the pin head that killed Bartello." She sunk to her knees. He picked her up and led her to the sofa. "The pin head showed what they call touch cells. Everything we touch, thousands of skin cells are transferred to that surface. DNA can be lifted from these cells if there are enough of them. Stone isn't sure if they have enough to identify DNA. He's waiting for the report. He already has made the assumption that whoever killed Bartello had to be real close and not a threat to him. Considering a hairpin, it could indicate it was a woman and that could be the way the weapon was concealed. Bartello was a strong family man and not known to entertain any women. The FBI would assume it was a business acquaintance of his. The walls are closing in Emily. Stone will make the connection. You'd be prime suspect because of Sam and his family connections with a rival organization."

"Oh my god, David!" Emily cried. "There's no way out."

"There is, just listen to me. We could go to Stone and the DA and tell them the whole story. For your information, you want immunity. I think you would have a good chance of getting it, because they want the Leone crime organization more than you. They could put you in witness protection. In a way, you would have eliminated both crime families single-handedly," he said.

"That's great consolation," she replied sarcastically. "Could you go with me?" she asked. "I don't think they would allow that" he said. "But you would be safe, and that's my biggest concern right now."

"I need time to sort this out," she said.

"You don't have much time," he said. "If they identify your DNA, it might be too late to broker a deal." She sat there, her world coming apart before her eyes. She was in a no win situation. "Emily, it's an easy decision. You don't have any loyalty to the Leones. You owe them nothing, so why put your safety on the line for them? The FBI can offer you protection. I'll talk to Stone on your behalf. If we get out in front of this, maybe we can minimize the damage." She stared at him. He really does care about me, she thought. I should have dropped the search and settled in with David. *I went too far. Now there's no turning back. My life changed forever when I committed murder. Will God ever forgive me?*

David set up the meeting with Stone the next day and didn't tell him why he wanted to meet. He just told him he wanted to run some information by him that was too delicate to discuss over the phone. He didn't tell him he was bringing Emily either. When they walked into Stone's office, he gave them a look of surprise. "I didn't expect you to bring anyone David, but it's a pleasure to see you again Emily. Please have a seat," Stone said motioning to a set of chairs. "Robert, we have known each other for years. What we are about to discuss is of the most confidential nature. Strictly off the record. I need your pledge and word that you will not divulge any of this information Emily is about to tell you without her written permission," David said. "Wow, David, directly to the point. This must be important," Stone said. "Let me tell my secretary to hold all my calls." He sat back and waited for Emily to proceed. "I killed Angelo Bartello," she blurted out. Stone was startled. David looked at her, never expecting her to be so direct. Tears filled her eyes. She sat with her head down. Stone looked at David for some explanation. David just stared back expressionless. "Tell me again, what did you just say?" asked Stone.

"I said I am responsible for the death of Bartello and his men." Emily began to pour out the whole story to Stone, weeping bitterly in the process. I was at the restaurant in the back office with Bartello when I took his life. It was a planned set up by me and the Leone family. Alex Leone and his men made sure there were no witnesses. Alberto waited for me at the back door to drive me away. It was a plan conceived to protect me and the Leone family from any backlash by the Bartello organization, who the Leones believed were responsible for the attempt on Frank's life. Sam is dead. They tortured him. Done by the hands of the Bartello family. Sam is buried in an unmarked grave. The Leones told me they would take me to his grave site. They recovered his body in Mexico after he had been held captive by a Mexican cartel, instigated by the Bartellos, to be used against his own family. The Leones convinced me that my life would be in constant danger. I was the only one who could get close enough to Bartello to kill him. I used a metal hairpin. They knew I would be searched, so Alex came up with the idea of a metal pin concealed in my hair. I had to get close enough to stab him in the eye." She stopped to gain her composure and continued after a brief moment. She stopped again and her eyes filled with tears. "I did it!" she exclaimed. "I wanted revenge for Sam. Now, I don't know what I want." Stone shifted in his chair. He looked at David in dismay. He didn't know what to say. After a long silence, David was the first to speak. "Well, Robert, what do you think?" "Are you kidding me? You just came in and dropped a bomb shell." Stone looked at Emily and said, "What do you want for this testimony?"

"She wants complete immunity for her to testify against the Leones!" David exclaimed. "I can't make that decision" said Stone. "But you know who can" replied David. Stone looked at Emily again. "Are you willing to take the witness stand under oath, in open court, in front of the Leones?" asked Stone. "If she gets her deal" answered David. Emily shook her head in agreement. "Do you suspect the Leones have any idea what you are about to do?" asked Stone. "I think they are planning to eliminate a liability. They have no reason to let me live. I'm no longer Sam's wife. They offered to help me relocate and fund my retirement. I think once I'm out of everyone's sight, I'll disappear permanently. Their afraid I'll crack and tell all I know. Or you guys would keep investigating until you turn something up. I'm the only one who could verify that they were involved in the murders. As far as I know, no one else in their family or organization knows who was there except Alberto, Alex, and Frank. David convinced me that I would be looking over my shoulder the rest of my life. He encouraged me to come here. I made a mistake I can't take back, so I had to confront my sin, ask for mercy." Emily said. Stone was amazed at her strength to see this through. "We need to put you under protective custody as soon as possible before the Leones suspect anything. I'll call an emergency meeting with the DA and the state attorney general," Stone said. "I hope they take this more seriously," said David, "than they did before, when they turned down a deal that would have prevented all this. Bartello would be alive and under indictment and we wouldn't be sitting here now, discussing Emily's future." "Be careful," Stone said. "Not a word of this to anyone. If this leaks out, you would be in grave danger. Stay with David until we get some authorizations to proceed. If they plan to get rid of you, they would pick up on any movements you make. They may also know you are here now if you're being followed. Go to work like nothing has changed. I will assign an undercover detail to watch you. As soon as I can get an answer, I'll call David. Your phone could be monitored."

They left Stone's office and headed home. "Do you think Stone can get me a deal?" Emily asked. "I think you made the right decision to try for one" answered David. "You gave him some compelling evidence. I've known him for a long time. His word is good. If he can't, he won't divulge that the information came from you." He kept checking his mirrors to see if any strange cars were following them. "The Leones know we are together, so it won't raise any suspicions if you stay with me. Stone will put a watch on your house also. I think it's too early for the Leones to act now. I think they will wait till you leave town before they do anything, if that is their plan to get you out of the way." David changed the subject, "You can stop at your house in the morning on your way to work. Tonight, let's go to my place and try to forget this for tonight and enjoy a quiet dinner."

Emily woke up early and took a shower. She had a change of clothes she brought the last time she stayed at his apartment. She poured herself a cup of coffee when David came into the kitchen. He looked like she felt. He probably didn't sleep well either. "What are your plans for the day?" she asked. "I'm going to go to my office and wait for Stone to call. I'll probably sift through some of my cases that are pending. I got to start making some money again, now that you're not a paying client anymore." She leaned over and kissed him tenderly. "Thank you for being here for me and believing in me. Most men would have run the other way when they learned what I did. You're a good man, David. You deserve better than to be saddled with my problems. I hope I can repay you. I would like the opportunity to make you the happiest man alive."

"I hope we both live to see that day," David replied.

CHAPTER FORTY-TWO

David drove up to his office and noticed something was wrong. His office door was ajar. He opened the door and saw that his office had been turned. His files from his desk were scattered on the floor. All the drawers of his desk and file cabinets were open and ransacked. Who would do this, an angry husband perhaps? This never happened before. Was this a burglary? But why? There was nothing of value. The only piece of equipment he had was a computer and it was still there. Someone must have been after information. He checked his computer and saw it had been hacked. What were they looking for? He called Emily. "Are you okay?" he asked. "Yes" she said. "What's wrong?" She could tell by his voice he was a bit distressed. "Someone broke into my office and turned the place out."

"O David," she moaned, "do you think the Leones are on to us and were looking for any information you might have on them? Maybe they are trying to erase any evidence you may have. They know you were investigating Sam's case with me. They may think you found something they don't want out about Sam and their family. Did you call Stone?" she asked.

"Don't panic yet," he said. "It could be a disgruntled client." He didn't want to alarm her and trigger a reaction if someone were observing her. "I just wanted to make sure you are okay. I'll get to the bottom of this, so don't worry, I'll talk to you later."

He spent the morning cleaning up the mess the break-in caused. He went through his computer to see what files were tampered with. He hadn't shut down his computer in days, so whoever broke in, had easy access to all his files. The last one opened was Emily's. He couldn't remember if he was in it last or if someone else was. The only thing the file contained was her name, address, and several entries he made from time to time. Then he saw it. He had Joey Pataglia and Angelo Bartello's name's listed. Also the Labella Italian Restaurant address. Were the Leones checking to see how much David knew or how much Emily told him? He called Stone's cell. When he didn't pick up, he left the 911 number. Stone called right back. "I'm in a meeting. What's wrong?"

"My office was broken into and I think it was the Leones behind it. My computer was on and Emily's file was opened. They were looking for something and I think they found it. My connection to the Bartello family. They know I know who they are. I have the names of Joey Pataglia and Angelo Bartello listed along with the address of the Labella Italian Restaurant. I think they are trying to figure out what I know and what Emily has told me. I may be next on their list. We have to move fast."

"I'm meeting with the DA right now. I'll call you back," replied Stone.

"Look," Stone said, "I told you it's a reliable source, but I'm not giving any names till I am assured of a deal. You want the Leone family, I can give them to you on a platter. Forget RICO charges. I can get them on first degree murder, conspiracy to murder, and deadly assault with a firearm. What else do you want?"

"You want complete immunity for your source, which means they must have had an active part in the murders. Will they testify in open court?" said the DA. "They assured me that they would with immunity and witness protection relocation. We would have to hide them after the indictment and during the trial," said Stone. "Would they summit to a lie detector test?" asked the DA. "I'm sure they would. They realize that's protocol under these circumstances" answered Stone. The DA turned to his assistant, "Have the proper documents drawn up and send them to Mr. Stone." He turned back to Stone, "I hope this doesn't blow up in our face. If this person participated in the actual murders, it could get dicey. They have the most expensive attorneys in the state. Will your witness hold up in court?"

"I believe so," Stone said. "Well, I'm looking forward to meeting with these witnesses. My office will get back with you, Robert, as soon as your people sign all the paper work, we'll set up a meeting. Have a nice day."

Stone was relieved the meeting went well. The hard part will be selling the DA on her credibility. Once he hears her story, he has to make the decision to go forward with the evidence she provides. Her rights will still be protected under the agreement. If he deems the evidence is not enough to prosecute, she can't be indicted under her immunity agreement. Life could get rougher for her though, because she would have exposed herself as an accomplice, and if it leaked out that she talked to the FBI, she would be in extreme danger. He called David to tell him the good news. "We have a deal" Stone told David. "The paper work is being drawn up and they will get it to me for Emily to sign. Does she know a good lawyer she can trust?"

"Good question. Do you think she needs one at this point?" asked David. "Yes, I do. I trust Jason White, the attorney general, we go back a long way. The district attorney, John Decker, I've worked with in the past. He's a rising star in the political arena. This case could propel him to the top, if he can secure a conviction. However, for her protection, she probably needs a representative to make sure all the t's are crossed and the i's dotted. Her life is at stake, as you well know. We don't need this coming back on us if we make a mistake," said Stone. "I'll talk to her and find out. It has to be someone who is above reproach," David replied. David called Emily. They had developed a secret code in case her phone was bugged. "Can you meet me at our favorite place after school?"

CHAPTER FORTY-THREE

David was waiting on the picnic bench in the park, where they had always enjoyed sitting and just talking. She came up behind him and kissed his neck. He was in deep thought and was a little startled. He turned and hugged her, then gave her a long passionate kiss. "Wow," she said, "it must be good news."

"Sit down Emily, they accepted the deal. The papers are being drawn up as we speak. When Stone gets them, he will call me. You need a good, trust worthy attorney to look over the documents and be your representative," he said. "But what about you and Stone? I trust you both."

"That's not good enough" he replied. "We are not lawyers. Your rights and your life depend on these conditions. Everything must be done to protect you," he said. "What about you? Where does this leave you in all this? Are you in danger? After all, your office was ransacked for a reason. Don't you need protection? Once the Leones find out what I'm doing, they may come after you. They know we are together," she said. "I'll talk to Stone about that later," he said. "For now, your safety is the big concern. Now, about a lawyer. Do you know any who you trust?" he asked. "No, the only legal contacts I know of were the ones Sam dealt with in real estate." David thought for a moment. "Maybe Stone will help us out. He may know an attorney who worked in the DA's office and now has their own practice. He would know the inner workings of the DA's department."

CHAPTER FORTY-FOUR

Frank Leone was feeling better and was able to walk. He was still restricted to the house. His personal physician came every day to check on his progress. There was no permanent brain damage. He suffered an occasional severe headache, but the doctor told him this was normal under the circumstances. It would pass in time. He was having his morning coffee with Alberto, going over recent events. "Did anything turn up in the private eye's office?"

"Not much," replied Alberto. "We did find her file and notes he had on his computer. He had Joey Pataglia and Angelo Bartello's names listed. He was apparently working on connecting them to Sam' disappearance. He also knows who we are. He could be a liability, if he starts snooping around our activities. Do you still want to go through with the deal we offered Emily?" Alberto asked.

"Of course. We need to get her as far away as possible," said Frank.

"Do you trust her?" asked Alberto.

"No! Not by a long shot. I don't know her to trust her. She's family but has no loyalty to us. We need to stick with our plan to get her out of town and make her silent forever," said Frank.

"It seems such a shame to do that to Sam's wife and a nice young lady," Alberto said. "It was your stupid idea to get her involved in the first place!" shouted Frank. "What were you and Alex thinking?" Frank stopped and lowered his head. He felt another headache coming on. He finished his coffee in silence and prayed his sister and Sam would forgive him. Too many other people's lives and well-being depended on Frank's decision. He had to protect the Family. This was one of the hardest decisions he'd ever make.

David had called Stone to inquire about an attorney for Emily. Stone did some research and called him back. "I talked to an attorney I knew when he worked for Jason White, when Jason was the DA. He was always very thorough and detail oriented. His name is Henry Cooper, but goes by Harry. He has his own law practice now and does a lot of public defending pro bono. He's known as the little man's attorney. He takes cases against major corporations and the government. Defending the rights of the less fortunate is his slogan. He's been very successful and is well known. He could be the perfect fit for Emily's situation. I told him she may be giving him a call. I didn't give him a lot of detail, but I could sense he was intrigued. Here's his number. Tell her to mention my name to refresh his memory. Good luck. Let me know if it works out. I'll call you when I get the papers," said Stone.

CHAPTER FORTY-FIVE

David and Emily walked into Clark Tower and took the elevator to the seventh floor. They exited the elevator and saw the door to Henry Cooper's office at the end of the hall. They opened the door and were greeted by a cheerful receptionist who invited them in. She sat behind a small counter and confirmed their names. "Would you like something to drink?" she asked. "Harry will be with you shortly."

"No, thank you," they replied. "Please have a seat, and I'll let him know you're here," the receptionist said as she walked toward the back to let Cooper know they were here. The waiting room was small, and quaint. No one else was waiting. Every wall had a unique painting. It had a homey feel, as opposed to the cold, professional law offices David had been in. A tall, slim, man, came over to introduce himself. "My name is Harry Cooper. You must be Emily Carson. It's a pleasure to meet you." He turned to David and said, "You must be David Kimbro. A friend of Robert Stone is a friend of mine. Please come into my office" He was well dressed in a suit and tie. His shoes were shiny and matched his suit. His hair was red and well groomed. He had a ruddy complexion. David imagined he had no trouble finding women. He did not wear a wedding ring. "Please make yourselves comfortable. Did my assistant offer you a refreshment?"

"Yes, and no," replied David, "we're good."

"Well, let's get down to business" Harry said. He looked at Emily. She was impressed with his calm and professional demeanor. Not to mention his good looks. "Tell me your story and why you need my assistance?" She handed him the documents provided by the DA's office. He glanced at them and put them aside. "I want to know all about the situation you now find yourself in."

"Are you familiar with the Bartello murder?" she asked.

"Yes, I am. Robert filled me in briefly. Tell me your part in all this."

"I was married to Sam Carson. He was a member of the Leone family. His mother was Frank Leone's sister. Frank is the boss of the Leone organized crime family. Sam was never involved with his families' activities. He was a real estate broker, who distanced himself from their name. He didn't bother with his family and never mentioned them to me. I only found out recently who his family was. Sam was kidnapped by the Bartello family and used against the Leones as a pawn to gain some operation control, which I have no idea why. He's dead now. Kidnapped and tortured. Left to die in a warehouse somewhere in Mexico," Emily stated. "How do you know all this?" Harry interrupted. "The Leones told me. I searched for Sam for months on end. The police closed the missing persons file on Sam, so I called David to help me. After the attempted assassination of Frank Leone failed, Angelo Bartello reached out to me to broker peace between the two families. How he knew I existed, I don't know. Apparently, they were watching me in case they needed leverage against the Leones. After I found out who Sam's family was, I went to them for some answers on Sam. I wanted to know if they had any information on his disappearance. I needed closure. Bartello told me he had information about Sam's disappearance and would tell me after the two families met. I brought a deal to Stone, which he took to Jason White, the attorney general. I was willing to tape the meeting between the two families, who would be discussing exchanging their political contacts by names, their sharing of drug territory, naming their drug distributors and dealers, but White refused the deal. It would have meant giving the Leones immunity for their part. They wanted Bartello out of the way, to draw out admissions from Bartello about his entire operation. The meeting never took place and Bartello never told me what he knew about Sam." Harry sat there taking in all the information. "Were you involved in the murder of Bartello?" he asked her. "While Frank was in the hospital,

Alberto Leone, Sam's other uncle, who I found out was the attorney or adviser for the family and, Alex, Sam's cousin, wanted to protect Frank and other members of the family from another attempt by Bartello. They approached me to take part in their assassination plan of Bartello. They needed someone to get close enough to Bartello to kill him. He was always well insulated from within and hard to get to. It had to be someone whom he considered not to be a threat. Alex came up with the idea. Since Bartello wanted a meeting, which the Leones thought would be a trap, they would have me meet with him first, under the pretense to finalize the terms of the exchange and decide on a neutral meeting place. Since Bartello thought me no threat, I could get close enough to take him out, as they say. We met in the office of the Labella Italian Restaurant. Alex said they would pat me down, just as a precaution. He devised a plan to use a long metal rod that looks like a hairpin. They would create a distraction in the restaurant, so I would get a chance to be alone with Bartello. I was full of frustration and vengeance. They played on my emotions. I agreed to deliver the fatal blow, a thrust through the eye to the brain. Alex instructed me on how to use all my force to make sure the rod penetrated into his brain. It was over in seconds. Bartello fell over dead. I ran out the back door to a waiting Alberto, who drove me away. Alex and his men made sure there were no witnesses, so no one could identify me."

"How did you get the pin in without detection?" asked Harry. "I hid the pin in my hair. It was a perfect plan" Emily explained. "Easy to execute."

"So you engaged in premeditated murder? How did it feel to take a man's life?" Harry asked firmly. Emily began to squirm in her chair. Tears streamed down her face. "It was like a blur. It was like an out of body experience. I regret it, I always will, and it's something I'll carry with me for the rest of my life."

"So what made you decide to turn states evidence against the Leones?"

"I think they want to eliminate me. I pose a threat. I am the only one who can identify them as the masterminds behind the slayings. I'm a loose end. They made a proposition to me. They would pay my expenses for me to leave town and not come back. It would be too risky to do anything to me here, but if I left, no one would be the wiser if I disappeared. Since Sam is dead, I'm not connected to the family anymore."

"Do you know were Sam's body is?" asked Harry. "Alberto said he would take me to his grave site. It's unmarked, so no one will know he's dead, so there's no questions asked. They don't want to open that investigation. When I leave town they said they'll show me."

"Do you think they suspect that you will betray them?" Harry asked. "I think they have already betrayed me and are plotting my demise," she answered. "What evidence do you have to place Alberto and Alex at the crime scene?"

"None that I know of."

"Well, if you don't, then it's going to be your word against theirs. In essence, you're admitting to a crime and place yourself there, you have no proof that anyone else was there, but you are saying you didn't act alone. Do you see my point? This deal by the DA's office is great, but the burden of proof lies in their lap. Your credibility is the only thing they'll have to work with. If you go through with this and lose, you'll be marked forever. Not to mention exposure to the Leone family. Think back to that night and try to remember anything that could tie them in. Any little detail. Who drove the getaway car? Was there anyone else in the car with you?" asked Cooper.

"Alberto drove. We were alone," Emily said. "Did you see anyone else, besides Bartello's men when you ran out the back door?" asked Harry. "Yes, I saw Alex and one of his men. I heard breaking glass and gun shots as I was running. I looked back and that's when I saw Alex."

"When you were in the car, did Alberto use his cell phone?" asked Harry.

"Yes, I think he talked to Alex for a few seconds," replied Emily.

"Do you remember what he said?"

"He asked if everyone was accounted for," she said.

"Then what?" asked Harry.

"He hung up," Emily replied.

David came out of his chair with excitement. Being a private investigator for years, he knew their phone records could place them both in the area. As smart as some criminals are, they sometimes make the slightest mistakes.

"Is this a good thing?" she asked after witnessing David's reaction.

"It could be. Emily, let me review the documents from the DA's office."

"Does this mean you will be my legal advisor during the whole process?" Emily asked. "The DA's office will handle the case after you sign the paper work. I can be at the initial meeting with the DA. They will want your statement and the entire story. They'll grill you pretty hard to make sure you are able to stand up in court and under depositions from the Leones' family lawyers," said David. "Can you review the documents now, so she can move on before anything else transpires?" David asked.

"Why don't you go get something to eat or drink? I'll look them over. Come back in an hour or so." Harry stood up and shook Emily's hand and she thanked him for seeing her.

"What now David?"

"Well, we wait and see what Harry thinks of the documents. If he recommends you sign them, then the games begin. You'll take them to the DA and meet to tell them all you know," said David. "What if the DA is not able to get an indictment? What happens to my life then?" asked Emily. "We'll cross that bridge when we come to it. Are you getting cold feet?"

"No, I want to see this through. I guess I don't have much of a future either way," replied Emily.

They went back to Cooper's office and waited for him to call them in. "Harry's ready for you. You may go back to his office." Harry stood up to greet them. "Please sit. I reviewed the documents and they seem to be in order. From my experience working at the DA's office, the immunity deals are pretty standard. What it says is you agree to testify and be a witness in court for the prosecution of Frank, Alberto, and Alex Leone. In exchange for your testimony, you will be exonerated from any charges pertaining to the case. Let me explain what this means. Immunity from the law is a status that makes a person essentially free from legal matters. Immunity in your case means that you do not have to be liable for damages or punished for any crime you committed in this case. State and federal statures may grant witnesses immunity from prosecution for the use of their testimony in court or before a grand jury. You will probably have to appear in both. The reason to grant you immunity is because your testimony is very valuable to the goals of crime prevention and serving justice, that the promise of allowing you to go unpunished is a fair trade. In this case, your testimony could help law enforcement to take down and destroy an entire illegal crime organization. For your cooperation, the prosecuting DA has granted you what's called a transactional immunity. This means you are completely immunized from prosecution for any offence to which the testimony relates. Do you have any questions?" Emily sat, trying to digest everything Harry just said. She looked at David. "Sounds like you're pretty much covered," David said. She looked back at Harry. "Where do I sign?"

Harry notarized the documents, sealed them, and had them couriered to John Decker. He told Emily he would call her as soon as Decker could meet with them. Harry hoped Emily was strong enough to withstand the pressure the lawyers were going to put her under. Her immunity deal was a strong one, especially with the transactional immunity clause. He decided he would go pro bono on this one. This case could help his profile. Besides, he felt sorry for her. She was a victim of manipulation, as he found in a lot of his cases. He always had a soft spot for attractive women, and she was quite stunning. He was looking forward to working with her.

Decker called Harry as soon as he opened the sealed documents. "When can we meet?" he asked Harry. "I'm free tomorrow afternoon," Harry replied. "Good," said Decker. "Get her in here. I am anxious to hear what she has to say."

"You will be quite surprised by what she can tell you. See you tomorrow," he said. Harry called Emily immediately. "We're on for tomorrow. I just hung up with Decker. We meet at two o'clock tomorrow afternoon. Can you be there?"

"Can I bring David?" Emily asked.

"Emily, that would suggest he had information concerning your actions, which could make him out as an accomplice to the murders. I think he would realize that. He shouldn't even be mentioned, except as the private investigator you hired, if it even comes up. Just prepare yourself to tell the whole story you related to me. You'll be under oath and recorded, so think very carefully when speaking. Be prepared to be cross examined, as if you were in a court room. Decker needs to know you're a credible witness," Harry told her. She hung up and called David. "I just got a call from Harry Cooper. The meeting with the DA is tomorrow afternoon. He said you couldn't be there. It could incriminate you as an accomplice, having knowledge of the circumstances," Emily said. "I figured that. I hadn't planned on attending for that reason anyway. You'll do fine. You don't need me there."

"You're wrong about that David, I always need you."

CHAPTER FORTY-SIX

Emily was waiting in the lobby of the Federal Building, where the DA's office is located, when Harry walked in. When he saw her, he immediately went over to greet her. "Hi Emily, are you ready for this?" Harry asked her as he gently placed his hand on her shoulder. "As ready as I'll ever be" she responded. "Let's go then," and they proceeded to Decker's office on the fifth floor. John Decker was a short, stocky, middle aged man who wore a wrinkled suit and thick glasses. He looked like he never slept and drank too much coffee. "How are you Mrs. Carson and hello to you too Harry. You just can't stay away, can you? Do you want your old job back?" Decker said as he playfully slapped Harry on the back. "No, I'm quite happy with where I'm at now," said Harry. Decker looked at Emily and said "I can see why. Please have a seat. Anyone want something to drink before we get started?" He sat across from Emily. "I have your signed documents so we can proceed with your testimony. My assistant will be transcribing your statements and we will also record you testimony. Do you consent to this Mrs. Carson?" asked Decker. "Yes," replied Emily. "Then let's begin. Tell me about your whole connection to the Leone family and all the events that occurred."

"First, let me begin at the end and work through the details. I killed Angelo Bartello and was there when Alex Leone murdered Bartello's men at the Labella Italian Restaurant." Harry looked at Decker to see his reaction. Decker never batted an eye. He just stared at Emily and told her to continue. Over the next hour, she reiterated all the events of the night of Bartello's death and what lead up to it.

"Let me see if I understand what you're telling me. You met Angelo Bartello at the restaurant with the sole purpose of carrying out a plan to murder Bartello? Alex and Alberto Leone developed the plan for you to kill Bartello. You delivered the death blow to Bartello, under their instructions. Is that correct?"

"Yes," Emily replied. For the next hour, Decker had Emily go over and over her story, periodically interrupting her for her to repeat herself. "What proof do you have that you didn't act alone?" Decker asked her. "How can we verify that Alex and Alberto were with you at the scene? You had cause and motive to carry out the assassination yourself. Is that not true?"

"Yes," she answered. "The Leones played on my emotions. They knew I was vulnerable and made me feel I was unsafe as long as Bartello was alive. I realized after I did it that I was only being used" Harry was silent the whole time Emily was giving her testimony. "John" he said. "May I inject something?" Decker looked at him with a puzzled look. "What is it?"

"You asked her if she had any evidence that would place the Leones at the crime scene," said Harry. "Yes, and?" Decker replied. Harry continued. "She said that Alberto made a call after she got in the car." Decker's demeanor changed. He turned to Emily and said, "Tell me about the phone call."

"I think he called Alex."

"What did he say?"

"He asked if everyone was accounted for. That was it," Emily said. Decker looked at Harry. "What do you think he meant by that?"

"I guess he meant all Bartello's men. They said they couldn't have any witnesses," said Emily." I guess they didn't count on you," commented Decker. "Does this make a difference John?" asked Harry. "Can you use the phone call to place them in the area?"

"Possibly. The FBI contends that their experts can trace the whereabouts of a suspect by returning to the crime scene and testing the strength and range of individual towers. They use it to place a suspect at the scene. The FBI and the local police maintain that they can place a suspect in a particular area because a cell phone, either making a call or receiving one, usually selects the closest tower with the strongest signal and most towers have a range of no more than a two mile range. Most judges rule its admissible evidence. A good attorney may challenge this technology. We would probably look for the GPS and try to pin point locations. This may be enough to force the Leones' hand to want to seek a plea bargain. They are old and may not want to take the chance of spending out their years in prison. Right now that's all we have. Emily's testimony and the cell call. We would need to sell her story to a jury. I think we can get an indictment from the Grand Jury. Then it goes to civil court. It's a long shot, but worth a try. I'm going to consult with Jason White on this one. I'll also get Stone's department to check the cell phone activity." Decker hesitated for a few seconds. "You said something else that caught my attention. You stated that you saw Alex as you were running to the back door. You said you heard gun shots and broken glass. Is that correct?"

"Yes I did," replied Emily. "Was he standing there or moving around?"

"He was moving quickly. I just caught a glimpse of him." Harry saw the look on Decker's face. "What are you thinking?" he asked. "I remember the crime scene. There was shattered glass on the floor of the restaurant. The car was protruding half way through the front window. If Alex stepped in any of the broken glass, we can place him at the scene."

"How?" asked Emily.

"There is such a thing as trace evidence" Decker answered. "The theory implies that a criminal will leave trace and take away trace evidence when at a crime scene. Trace evidence refers to minute samples of a substance, such as fibers, hair, glass fragments, and paint chips. Pieces of broken glass can be physically reconstructed to form the original object or pane. Due to the nature of glass, it may be possible to determine whether two pieces originated from the same source. Tiny shards of glass can be found on the bottoms of the shoes, particularly if Alex was running or standing in the vicinity of where the glass was smashed. The fragments will cling to clothing or footwear, even after washing. We can get a search warrant and test all his footwear." Decker looked at his watch. "I think we need to break for a while. I'm sure you could use one about now, Mrs. Carson. We'll pick this up again later. Speak to no one about this meeting. I need to make some calls and get things moving. I'm going to set up a detail to watch you, for protection, until we make our move against the Leones. Just go about your day as if nothing's changed." He stood up to shake her hand. "Harry, can you stick around for a moment?" Emily left and Harry sat back down. "Do you believe her story?" Decker asked. "It's more important that you do," answered Harry. "I think she's telling the truth. Why would she admit to a murder, if it were not true?"

"Well," said Decker, "it could be she's worried she'll be found out and wants to shift the responsibility and bring someone down with her. It could be guilt. It could be remorse. But I have to agree with you. She couldn't have planned this without professional help. It was too clean just to be her. Hopefully we can get more evidence then just her witness testimony."

"When are you going to put her under witness protection?" asked Harry. "As soon as I get Judge Wilson to issue a search warrant of Alex Leone's home. I'll have Stone's men handle the search. And Harry, don't get involved with this one. She wouldn't be good for your career."

Emily was exhausted. She drove home and poured herself a glass of red wine. She wished David could have been at the meeting. She missed him now. She thought about calling him but, she needed to lie down and relax. It had been a long, trying experience. Tomorrow may be her last day of freedom. The little she knew of Decker, one thing was for sure, he was a man of action. She expected to be hauled away to a secret hiding place. She may never be able to be with David alone again. She grabbed her phone and called him. "I've been waiting to hear from you" he said. "How did it go?"

"I'll tell you as soon as you can get here. Please hurry, I miss you."

Emily went to work the next day as usual. She felt a lot better after spending the night with David. He had a calming effect on her. He reassured her she made the right decision to come forward and testify against the Leone family. She couldn't live the rest of her life running or looking over her shoulder. She wanted all this to end so her and David could start a life together. She felt young and alive again when she was with him. He was her second chance at life.

Decker called Stone the next morning. "Robert, I just met with Emily Carson yesterday afternoon. I'm sure you already heard her testimony. I believe her story. I think she'll be a credible witness. She also revealed some interesting information that could place both Alberto and Alex Leone at the crime scene. She said when she ran out of Bartello's office she heard gun shots and glass shattering. She saw Alex in the restaurant for a split second. If he was there and stepped in the glass, he would have glass fragments on his shoes and maybe on his clothing. Also, the floor mats in his car could have traces of glass. Also, Alberto made a phone call when she got in the car. It sounded to her that he called Alex to see if the job was done. We have two sources to investigate for evidence. I'm waiting for Judge Wilson to sign the search warrant for Alex's house and his car. Can you check the phone records and see what you can come up with on Alberto? When I get the warrant, hopefully you can get some trace evidence from Alex."

Alex was just getting ready to have his morning coffee when Stone's men knocked on his door. He opened the door and saw five men with FBI jackets and IDs around their necks. They each had several empty boxes. "Mr. Leone? Alex Leone?"

"Yes, what's this all about?" asked Alex. "We have a search warrant for your house and your cars." He handed the warrant to Alex. "Please step aside and let my men in," said the agent in charge.

Alex was stunned and caught completely off guard. *What are they looking for?* he thought. They went directly to his bedroom and started going through his closet. One of the FBI men told Alex to remain in the kitchen and finish his coffee. He called Alberto and told him what was happening. "Stay calm. Do you know what they are looking for?" asked Alberto. "No, I don't have a clue."

"Then keep your mouth shut and observe what they take. I'll make some calls to see what's going on. You stay put till I call you." Alberto hung up and called his contact, who is a court clerk at the Federal Court Building. "I haven't heard or seen anything. If a warrant was issued, it didn't come through my office. I'll check and let you know." Alberto's mind raced. Did Emily beat them to the punch? If it had to do with Bartello's murder, there were no witnesses and no evidence to implicate him or Alex. It was a clean hit. No ballistics could be traced back to them. They used an untraceable gun. Alex got rid of the gun right away. I never even went in the building, only Alex. He wore gloves, so there can't be any finger prints. If someone saw us and got an ID on the cars, the police would have questioned us. Besides, the license plates were stolen. His phone rang. It was his court clerk contact. "I can't find anything on a warrant issued today or yesterday. If one was issued, as you say, on your brother, it had to be very confidential. Usually when this happens, it's so the party is not alerted to the search and the media won't be alerted. I don't know which judge would have been available to sign. It could be Judge Wilson. If it's the FBI, he usually works with the DA's office. That's all I can tell you." Alberto hung up and called Frank.

CHAPTER FORTY-SEVEN

The search of Alex's home and his car lasted for several hours. The FBI carted out at least ten boxes. Alex wouldn't be able to know what they took till they left and he could be free to move around in his house again. As soon as they left, he went straight to his bedroom. His closet was tossed and some of his clothes and all his shoes were gone. He had no idea what they found in his car. He called Alberto. "They took all my shoes!" he exclaimed. "What the hell is going on? Did you tell Frank?" Alex asked. "He's having a fit. He thinks we screwed up somehow on the Bartello situation," Alberto said. "How? We left nothing to implicate us?" said Alex. "We probably need to stop talking on the phones, in case we're being monitored" said Alberto. "Meet me at Frank's house in an hour."

Stone over saw the testing on Alex's shoes and clothing. The mat in Alex's car showed traces of shard glass. A pair of his shoes also had glass fragment on the soles. They were able to lift the fragments with adhesive tape. Very carefully lifting, the fragments stuck to the tape. The car mat was easy to collect the glass shards, because of the rough texture and groves. The next step was to match them to the glass collected from the restaurant floor. Even though the floor had been clean, it still left tiny fragments, which the FBI team was able to obtain. They made the match and sent the report to Decker. Stone's people were also able to pin point the location and time of the phone call Alberto made to Alex. The next step was to take the evidence to the grand jury.

Decker called Stone when he received the lab report from Alex's shoes and car mat. He decided to go to the grand jury, opposed to having a preliminary hearing. If he chose to have a preliminary hearing, he would have to convince a judge that he has enough evidence to secure a conviction. The Leones would have their lawyers present to contest his evidence. Also, during a preliminary hearing, their lawyers can see and cross-examine his witnesses, which gives the defense a good preview into his case. In grand jury proceedings, he only has to prove there's probable cause to believe a crime has occurred and the accused committed them. "I reserved time with the grand jury. I'll be presenting evidence of your finding along with testimony from Emily Carson. I don't want the Leones to know what evidence we have yet. The proceedings will be in secret and will be kept in strict confidence. I don't want any arrests made yet while I present my findings. If the grand jury chooses to indict, the trial will most likely start faster. Let's hope the grand jurors decide the evidence creates probable cause to believe the Leones committed the crimes charged against them and vote to return an indictment," said Decker.

"What about Emily, do we put her under witness protection?" asked Stone. "No, not yet" replied Decker. "I don't want the Leones on to her yet. Just continue to keep a watch on her. She's our star witness."

Frank, Alberto, and Alex met at Frank's home. Alex wore slippers. He hadn't had time to pick up a pair of shoes. "Why do you think they took your clothing and shoes?" Frank asked.

"I don't have a clue. If they are looking at me for the Bartello murder, I didn't have any blood on them. I was never that close to his men. I wasn't hit with splatter either, I was very careful."

"Did you leave any foot prints?" asked Frank. "It wasn't raining. The ground was dry. Besides the floor was carpet and tile. How could I leave prints?" asked Alex. "You never stepped in blood?" asked Frank. "No, I told you, I was never close. I knew they were dead. I put enough holes in them that I didn't have to go near them to check if they were dead. It can't be about Bartello and his men. It was too clean and with no witnesses and we left no evidence."

"Well, I guess we'll know soon enough" Frank replied.

Emily walked out of the school building and checked her cell phone. There was a message from John Decker to call his office. "Decker speaking."

"Hi, Mr. Decker, it's Emily Carson returning your call."

"I have news for you. Can you come to my office? I don't want to have a discussion on the phone?"

"When?" she asked.

"Can you come now?"

"Give me thirty minutes," she said. She was nervous and scared. The realization hit her. She was in deep, deeper than she ever imagined when she first started to search for Sam. She was going to stop at home, but she decided to go directly to his office. She wanted to hear what he had to say, and get it over with. It couldn't be good. Maybe they rescinded the deal for immunity. Twenty minutes later she walked into his office. His receptionist told her to go back to his office, he was expecting her. Decker stood up to greet her. "Thank you for coming on such short notice. Please have a seat. The reason I wanted to meet with you is I have good news. Robert Stone's office was able to secure some compelling evidence from Alex Leone's home. He found glass fragments on Alex's soles of his shoes and fragments of glass shards on his car's floor mat. They also identified the time and location of Alberto's call to Alex and tied it to the night of Bartello and his men's murders. With your testimony and the evidence we now have, I am going to present it to the grand jury. Due to the nature of your testimony, the proceedings to the grand jury will be private. When an indictment is handed down, which I feel very good about, we will then arrest the Leones on first degree murder and other charges. At that time you will enter the witness protection program. During the trial, if the Leones don't try to plea bargain, we will transport you back and forth to the trial. You will stay in an undisclosed location. The media will not be told about the grand jury hearing, but will besiege us during the trial. You will have to be there to give your testimony. Just tell them everything you told me. They will know you have immunity. We will sneak you in the back door under heavy coverage. No one will see you enter or leave. I don't want the Leone family to know what hit them till I can have them arrested. As you know, tell no one about this for your own safety. Since we feel your life may be in danger, I've asked for an emergency hearing to have the grand jury convene as quickly as possible. I will call you as soon as I get the day and time. Stone's men will continue to keep watch over you."

Emily drove home to a waiting David. He had cooked her dinner. She told him about her meeting with Decker. He held her as she talked. He knew if it went to trial, Emily would be even more miserable but it was too late to turn back. His job now was to comfort her and be her support for the days ahead.

A grand jury can consist of twelve to twenty-three people and is a body that investigates criminal conduct and is used to decide whether probable cause exists to support criminal charges. Grand juries hear cases from prosecutors all day long. Emily researched this information. When she entered the room, the jurors were seated in a college lecture type of setting. There was no judge present, just court officers and grand jury clerks. Decker met her and seated her next to himself. Decker told Emily that the grand jury proceedings are much more relaxed than normal court room proceedings. He told her the jurors have broad power to see and ask almost anything they would like. "Don't be shy. Answer any question they ask to the best of your ability. I'll present the charges and submit the evidence, including your testimony. Then, I'm sure they'll have many questions. Just relax and be cooperative. As I said, answer all their questions to the best of your ability." She took a deep breath and glanced at the jurors. She counted twenty-two. It was going to be a long day.

A week went by as everyone waited for the grand jury's decision. Things started to get back to normal for Emily. The hearing was very tense as she recounted all the events to the jurors. She sensed some of them were already judging her for her participation in the murders. Decker told her not to read too much into their reactions or lack of them. The only requirement is that probable cause exists to support the criminal charges and a two thirds approval to hand down an indictment. The Leones were in a quandary, trying to find out why a search of Alex's house was conducted. They didn't attempt to contact Emily. She worked every day as if nothing was going to change.

She continued her relationship with David and they were becoming closer and closer every day. She feared that she may have to go into hiding without him. Then, she got the call. "Emily, it's John Decker. We got a verdict. The grand jury just handed down an indictment." Her heart pounded. Now, a trial. She would be exposed to the world. She would forever be branded a murder. Her face will be all over the news. "How soon will the trial take place?" Emily asked.

"For now, I'm not letting the media know until the arrest warrants have been issued. One of the things we need to know to help our case is the location of where your husband is buried. You said you asked Alberto Leone to take you to where they buried your husband Sam. You also said they agreed to do this after Bartello was eliminated. Is that correct?" Decker asked.

"Yes, that's correct" she replied. "Then I need you to contact Alberto and remind him of his commitment to you. They should be under the pretense that you are accepting their offer to leave town. Call them and arrange this meeting, telling them you have tied up all your affairs and are ready to leave. They will probably welcome this arrangement. After the search of Alex's home, they probably figure the sooner they get rid of you the better."

Emily told David about the conversation with Decker. "I'm scared, David. What if they know what I'm doing and will kill me at the meeting? They could do it right there and bury me beside Sam."

"Stone has assured me that the Leones have no idea why the search was conducted at Alex's home," David told her. "He thinks they're confused or they would have made contact with you. Besides, the FBI will be monitoring your every move. Call the number Alberto gave you. Set up the meeting and get this whole ordeal over before something changes."

"You know I'll probably have to leave town after this. When they arrest him, I have to go into hiding till the trial starts. I won't be able to see you for who knows how long," Emily stated. "I know" he said. "Stone already informed me. That's all the more reason to get this over with," said David.

CHAPTER FORTY-EIGHT

Emily called Alberto the next day. "Alberto, this is Emily."

"I was expecting your call for a while now. We thought maybe you changed your mind about our deal," said Alberto. "No, on the contrary" she said. "I needed to get my affairs in order. I'd like to leave as soon as possible. You promised to take me to Sam's grave, remember?"

"Of course I do" he replied.

"When?" she responded. "Let me call you back" he said. Alberto called Frank and told him what Emily wanted. "If that's what it will take to have her leave town, then arrange it," Frank told him. "The sooner she is dealt with, we can relax."

Emily called Decker. "I made the call to Alberto. He's going to call me with the place and time."

"Make your preparations for leaving," he said. "It could be for a long time, depending on how soon I can get a court date. You will be escorted to your new safe house by the FBI. You realize even after the trial, it may be unsafe for you to come back. That's when you will go into the witness protection program, for your own safety." Decker told her. She hung up and started preparing for her new life.

Emily visited Sam's grave on her way out of town. She met Alberto and Alex at the gate of the family cemetery. She stood beside the unmarked area that was Sam's final resting place. No head stone or marker or even flowers. "Maybe someday we will be able to give Sam a proper headstone," Alberto said. "Frank would have liked to be here, but he is still not able to get around yet. He sends his condo-

lences, and wants you to know you can call if you ever need anything."
She had resigned from her teaching position. She said goodbye to all
her fellow teachers, friends, and students. She apologized for leaving
abruptly, but used the excuse that the pressure of not finding her
husband was too overwhelming. She needed some time to reorganize
her life. She turned the selling of her home over to a friend of Sam's
in the real estate business. The rest of her personal items and all her
furniture she placed in storage. She closed all her bank accounts and
had her mail sent to a post office box. The only regret she had was
leaving David. She knew he loved her and would stand by her, but
she couldn't take the chance that if she were charged for the murder
of Angelo Bartello, he could be implicated because of their relationship. She recalled how difficult it was to say goodbye to him. The FBI
followed her to the grave site and as she left with Alberto and Alex,
they moved in and arrested both of them. She turned her head away.
She could not look them in the eye as they realized she betrayed
them, just as they had planned to do to her. Someone was already at
Frank's front door with an arrest warrant. She now realized why Sam
had walked away from his family years ago.

Emily drove into town for the first time in eight years. She
still remembered that tragic night when she avenged her husband
Sam's death. She still thinks about him. Ten years of marriage. She'd
had numerous male friends since she'd been gone, but none worthy
enough to settle down with. They were either married, divorced, or
momma's boys. They served their purpose. She at least got immediate gratification in most of the affairs. Loneliness and lust will do
that to a girl. Even a couple of glasses of wine didn't do the trick
anymore. Only one lover in her life was genuine. She hadn't seen
or heard from him since she had to leave. Their relationship had to
end when she decided to take the Leone family's offer to leave town.
That started the arrest and conviction process. David wanted to go
with her, but she didn't want him to give up the life he built here.
Going into witness protection was not easy, giving up your life and
taking on a new one. As it turned out, Alberto and Alex worked
out a plea bargain with Decker. John Decker had such an impelling
case against them, that they agreed to turn states evidence against

their organized crime organization, which gave Decker a multiple win. Alberto was charged with volunteer manslaughter and received a ten-year sentence. Alex pleaded guilty to second degree murder and received a twenty-year sentence. They were charged under a Federal crime, which does not grant parole. They have to serve the entire sentence. They avoided the premeditated first-degree murder charge, which brought the death penalty. The case never went to trial, and she never had to testify in open court, for which she was grateful. She didn't know if her life would still be in danger, but something drew her back. Now, she was coming home, and her first quest would be to find David. She hoped she wasn't too late.

The End

ABOUT THE AUTHOR

Robert A. Frey was born in Pittsburgh, Pennsylvania. He grew up as part of a large family, with many aunts, uncles, and cousins whose relationships inspired him to write. He attended Robert Morris University, where he received a Bachelor's Degree in Business Administration. Later he attained a real estate brokers license, which enabled him to meet many people from many walks of life, which inspired him to write this book.

PSIA information can be obtained
www.ICGtesting.com
rinted in the USA
FOW02n0159300917
494FF

9 781640 826199

C
a
P
F
40